# 'Are these my basoomas I see before me?'

## Fab FINAL Confessions

### of Georgia Nicolson

**The Confessions of Georgia Nicolson:**

Angus, thongs and full-frontal snogging
'It's OK, I'm wearing really big knickers!'
'Knocked out by my nunga-nungas.'
'Dancing in my nuddy-pants!'
'...and that's when it fell off in my hand.'
'...then he ate my boy entrancers.'
'...startled by his furry shorts!'
'Luuurve is a many trousered thing...'
'Stop in the name of pants!'
'Are these my basoomas I see before me?'

Also available on tape and CD:
'...and that's when it fell off in my hand.'
'...then he ate my boy entrancers.'
'...startled by his furry shorts!'
'Luuurve is a many trousered thing...'
'Stop in the name of pants!'
'Are these my basoomas I see before me?'

# 'Are these my basoomas I see before me?'

## Fab FINAL Confessions
### of Georgia Nicolson

*Louise Rennison* ♥

HarperCollins *Children's Books*

Find out more about Georgia at www.georgianicolson.com

First published in Great Britain in hardback by HarperCollins *Children's Books* 2009
HarperCollins *Children's Books* is a division of HarperCollins*Publishers* Ltd,
77-85 Fulham Palace Road, Hammersmith, London W6 8JB

1

ISBN-13 978-0-00-727733-9

Printed and bound in England by
Clays Ltd, St Ives plc

**Mixed Sources**
Product group from well-managed
forests and other controlled sources
www.fsc.org  Cert no. SW-COC-1806
© 1996 Forest Stewardship Council

FSC is a non-profit international organisation established to promote the
responsible management of the world's forests. Products carrying the FSC
label are independently certified to assure consumers that they come
from forests that are managed to meet the social, economic and
ecological needs of present and future generations.

Find out more about HarperCollins and the environment at
www.harpercollins.co.uk/green

*In memory of the original Luuurve God with the big fat red Yorkshire legs:*
*Big Fat Bobbins.*

This is dedicated to you all.
I quite literally love you all.

p.s. I hope I love you as much as you love me.
But I can't worry about that now because that is life, isn't it?

p.p.s. Perhaps I love you more than you love me, which is a bit mean as I am bothering to dedicate this book to you.

# A Note from Georgia

Dear little chumettes,

As our lederhosen friends say, "Now ist zer time to say guten tag." I don't know why they say it, but they do. And frankly, I love them for it. All right, Germany may not be Billy Shakespeare land but any country that says spangelferkel instead of sausage is top with me, comedywise... although not holidaywise.

Where was I? Oh yes, saying goodbye. As you know, I have been working like a bee (two bees) to once more give you my all (oo-er) creativitositywise. And here it is, my final oeuvre. (Now you are being silly, you know I don't mean "here is my final egg", so stop messing about.) And you will be pleased to know, I think I have pulled it off. (Oo-er.) Stop it.

So this is my final (boo hoo) diary. It is, of course, packed with the usual combination of sophisticosity and snot dancing. But be warned, there are some exciting additions - Melanie's nunga-nungas make a big and unexpected appearance, as well as other twits in tights etc.

Some of you will laugh, some of you will cry, some of you may have a little accident in the piddly-diddly department. I don't know.

But I care.
A LOT.
I do.
And even though I am away laughing on a fast camel, you will always feel my luuurve.
Are you feeling it yet?
I am.

Georgia
xxxxx


p.s. I mean it about luuurving you all, little chums.

p.p.s. I am giving you telepathic hugs.

p.p.p.s. But not in a telepathically lezzie way.

p.p.p.p.s. And remember my advice to see you through the Georgia-less days ahead...
Snog on, snog on,
With hope in your heart,
And you'll never snog alone,
You'll never snog... alone.

you know you luuurve it, you cheeky Fräulein!

## Sunday September 18th

**9:00 a.m.**

Why. Oh why oh why?

**9:02 a.m.**

Why me?

**9:03 a.m.**

And I'll just say this. Why?

**9:04 a.m.**

One minute, I am the girlfriend of a Luuurve God, skipping around like a Sex Kitty on kittykat tablets and the next minute I am at Poo College, in Pooford. Doing a degree in Poonosity and *Merde*.

**9:10 a.m.**

Masimo, my Pizza-a-gogo Luuurve God, stropped off with the megahump last night. Not even stopping to say goodbye-io, or whatever they say in Pizza-a-gogo land. I may never know now.

**9:12 a.m.**

Why? Why oh why oh why?

**9:13 a.m.**

Just because I did a bit of harmless twisting with Dave the Laugh at the Stiff Dylans gig.

That's all.

**9:15 a.m.**

Is doing the twist such a crime?

Why would you get the Humpty Dumpty about that?

**9:16 a.m.**

I wouldn't mind, but he doesn't even know about the accidental snogging Dave the Laugh in the forest of red-bottomosity incident. Which I will never be mentioning this side of the grave.

**9:17 a.m.**

If he gets the numpty about a bit of twisting, what number on the Having the Hump Scale would he get to for accidental snogging?

**9:18 a.m.**

Perhaps Masimo has only got the overnight hump with me and he will be calling me soon.

**9:30 a.m.**

Oh joy unbounded. My vati has come barging into MY room. Which to be frank isn't big enough for him and his bottom.

I am pretending to be asleep.

Thirty seconds later

The gros vater said, "Quickly, quickly rise and shine."

I said, "Erm... Vati... it is Vati, isn't it? Can you go away and I will pretend I haven't noticed you breaking into my room without permission. Which incidentally you will never get. Goodbye."

He came over and ruffled my hair, which is technically assault. I could get on the blower to ChildLine.

Dad was still going on and on in his dadtastic way. As he ripped back my curtains, nearly blinding me, he was rubbing his hands together and saying, "Come on, let's have some family fun. Put your wellies on – we're off to the bird sanctuary."

That woke me up. He is deffo getting madder by the minute. And also he is wearing tight jeans. Surely there is some sort of law about that.

I said, "Dad, I am far too busy to go and look at budgies. Besides, I have seen one."

He didn't take any notice and went off. "I'll be revving up the funmobile. See you in five."

He was whistling "Sex bomb, sex bomb, I'm a sex bomb". Pornographic whistling. I will probably be scarred for life.

## Five minutes later

Oh, the embarrassmentosity of having a dad. He is revving up his clown "car". It sounds like a fat bloke revving up a sewing machine. Which it is really. He has painted a racing stripe down the side of his three-wheeled Reliant Robin. Even Grandad overtook the clown car the other day, and he wasn't even on his bike. He was just walking quite briskly. That is how pathetico the Robinmobile is.

## One minute later

Anyway, how can I be expected to go look at budgies when I may once more be a dumpee on the rack of luuurve.

## Four minutes later

Mum came mumming in.

I said, "Before you start, I'm not coming to look at budgies and that is *le* fact."

She said, "Hang on a minute, what are you doing here?"

I said, "Er, I live here."

She said, "You were supposed to be staying at Jas's though."

"Well... she was a bit... tired."

"You fell out then?"

"Maybe."

"What did you do to upset her?"

Oh, that's nice, isn't it? Nice and supportive.

"It was Saint Jas's fault actually, if you must know. She was the one who told me to do something when Masimo and Dave the Laugh nearly had fisticuffs at dawn. And then when I did do something she got the mega hump and a half with me and stropped off."

Mum came and sat on the edge of the bed. Oh Lord, now she had got interested. Drat.

She said, "Dave and Masimo were fighting?"

"Sort of."

"Why?"

"I don't know. Because I did a bit of ad-hoc twisting with Dave, and Masimo got the hump."

"So what did you do to stop them?"

"Well. I stepped in the middle of them and told them not to be silly."

Mum looked at me. "What did you actually say?"

"Stop in the name of pants."

Mum just looked at me again. She is like a seeing-eye dog.

I bumbled on. "But then Rosie started singing that crap song from *The Sound of Music* – 'The hills are alive with the sound of PANTS, with PANTS I have worn for a thousand years.' And the Ace Gang joined in and…"

"And?"

"Then Masimo just looked at me and he walked off. And not in a good way. In a having the full Humpty Dumpty way."

**10:30 a.m.**

The budgie lovers' "advice" is: "Don't be such a childish arse in future."

Thank you for that.

**10:40 a.m.**

At least I have the house to myself for a mope-a-thon. The Swiss Family Mad have roared off down the drive at three miles an hour. They'll be at the end of our street by tomorrow if they're lucky and have a following wind.

**10:45 a.m.**

I'm not phoning Jas because she was so grumpy with me last night for no reason.

**Five minutes later**
I think I may hate her actually.

**Two minutes later**
So in a nutshell. My so-called bestie hates me and thinks I am the Whore of Babylon and my boyfriend may hate me, even though he doesn't know the reason why he should hate me.

**Six minutes later**
It is sooooo boring moping.

**11:10 a.m.**
Masimo still hasn't phoned me. I can't stand this silence a moment longer. I am going to call an emergency Ace Gang meeting.

**11:30 a.m.**
Rang Jools, Ellen, Rosie, Mabs and Honor.

**11:45 a.m.**
I have arranged to meet the Ace Gang, with the exception of

you know who, at 2:00 p.m. in the park. I wanted to meet at mine, but the rest of them want to watch the footie match. They are obsessed with boys.

**11:50 a.m.**
I am just going to tell them all the whole truth and see what they say. Just come clean about the whole situation. Make a fresh start with my bestie mates. Truth is, after all, the cornerstone of friendship.

**11:52 a.m.**
Well, when I say the whole truth, I will obviously not be mentioning the thing that I am not mentioning this side of the grave. And which I have forgotten about, to tell you the truth.

**1:30 p.m.**
I seem to be working my way through the famous "losing it" scale. I have gone from merely having a spaz attack to being now on the edge of a complete nervy b. What if Masimo is actually at the footie match and ignores me?

What can I do?

I ask myself the question, "What would Baby Jesus do in these circumstances?"

One minute later

Of course! I must make myself irresistible to the Luuurve God by applying as much mascara as is humanly possible.

1:32 p.m.

When I went into the bathroom, Angus was sitting on the loo seat. He just looked at me when I came in and then half shut his eyes, like a halfwit cat.

I said, "Oy, what are you doing in here?"

He yawned and then he put his paw on the loo handle. Like he was flushing it.

What fresh hell?

Surely he isn't pooing in the loo?

He jumped down and skittered off out at about a million miles an hour.

How weird.

I wonder if being run over has affected his brain.

Mind you, I read about the Moscow State Circus and

they've got some cats who can pull a carriage and play chess at the same time.

Maybe I could get Angus a job in the Russian circus displaying his pulling-the-loo-handle skills.

The Russian *volk* might quite like that.

You never know.

**1:40 p.m.**
Oh, bloody hell, he's been in my make-up bag again.

Why would a cat eat lip gloss?

**1:45 p.m.**
OK, I am ready to get entrancing and alluring. I am wearing jeans and a skinny jummie, and because I am off to watch a footie match, I've put my hair into a little ponytail. *Très sportif*. It gives me a casual, sporty air.

I may wear my shades to add to my mysterious "uuumph" quality.

**1:46 p.m.**
Just a hint of "uuumph" but not ummphy in the "oy, you slaaaag" sort of way.

When I arrived at our usual meeting place underneath the big chestnut tree, Sven and Rosie were there. Practically eating each other. Do they ever stop snogging?

Rosie knew I was there because she waved her hand at me.

Eventually, I went: "Helllloooooooo" for a bit until they came up for air.

Rosie took out her chuddie and said, "*Bonsoir*, sensation-seeker."

Sven leaped to his feet and picked me up (thank God I had my jeans on) and started carrying me around singing, "Oh *ja*, oh *ja*! The hills are alive wiv zer pants, hahaha, oh *ja* pants!!!"

I said to Rosie, who was reapplying her lippy, "Rosie, make him put me down..."

Rosie said, "Down, boy."

He put me down and licked Rosie's face before he ambled off like Lug the Larger to the footie field.

I said to her, "How does this happen? One minute I've got more boyfriends than I can shake a stick at and the next minute I am the Leper of Rheims."

Rosie looked at me and put her armey round me. "Would you like to sit on my knee for a bit? You like that."

I just looked at her.

## Five minutes later

Jools, Mabs, Hons and Ellen arrived.

The meeting began with the official passing around of the Midget Gems. Then we discussed how to make Masimo stop having the hump and start having the Horn.

## Twenty minutes later

This is our cunning plan.

I have to be nice.

That is it.

I have to be nicey girl on legs for as long as it takes to make Masimo luuurve me again.

The Ace Gang is going to help by only saying really, really nice things about me.

There was a bit of a verging on the "mentioning the thing that I will not be mentioning this side of the grave" when Ellen said, "Masimo, I mean, he like... well, he got the hump when... er... the twisting, or maybe Dave the Laugh or something... erm."

Jools said, "Ah yes, he didn't like you dancing like a fool with Dave the Laugh, did he?"

Mabs said, "It's his hot Pizza-a-gogo blood. They get vair jealous."

Rosie said, "You might have to eschew Dave the Laugh with a firm hand for a bit."

OK, well, I can knock it on the head laaarfwise with the Hornmeister.

It's a shame.

But ho hum pig's bum.

### Two minutes later

But what if I don't even get the chance to be nicey-nice girl?

What if Masimo doesn't get in touch with me again?

I fear the tensionosity will drive me to not only having a complete nervy b. but I might also go ballisticisimus.

### 2:45 p.m.

The lads are arriving, getting their boots on and shouting WUBBISH. They don't seem to be able to just say "Hello" to each other. It's all "Aaaaaaah, you're shit!" and "On my head." "Hello, you complete tosser." Quite, quite weird. No sign of Dave the Laugh – perhaps he's not playing today. Just as well really.

**2:50 p.m.**
Sven has put two footballs down the front of his shirt and is swaying around like a girl. A girl nearly two metres tall, with massive hairy legs and the beginnings of a goatee.

Rosie said, "I think I'm on the turn. Svenetta is bringing out my inner lesbian."

Oh good, everyone has gone bonkers. Excellent.

I said, "Rosie, will you promise not to mention your inner lezzie if Masimo turns up?"

Rosie winked at me. "I'll try, but don't you start waggling your nungas about, you little minx."

Do you see what I mean? This is exactly what I am trying to avoid.

**Five minutes later**
Dom, Edward, Rollo, Declan, Sven and two others of the Stiff Dylans are all running around "limbering up".

Meanwhile, it's Cosmetic Headquarters behind our tree. In principal, I think you should be loved for yourself, and your soul shines through even if you haven't got mascara on. I know this is what Baby Jesus says and he is renowned for never having worn mascara. So, in principal, I think you should just be yourself, but in practice, I am applying just a tad more mascara.

Speaking of which, Ellen is in such a ditherama about seeing Declan that she has actually got some mascara on her teeth. How?

Two minutes later

Jas'n'Tom have turned up.

Oh yes. Here comes Miss Prissy Knickers herself. And her boyfriend, Hunky. She caught sight of us and shouted over, "Hi, Rosie, hi, Ellen, Mabs, Jools, Hons..."

She deliberately didn't say hello to me. How childish.

Two could play at that game.

I shouted out, "Hi, Hunky!" Tom waved at me and went off.

Then I noticed that Jas was not alone. She had brought two of her stuffed owls with her. And they had got little football hats and scarves on.

How pathetico.

I shouted, "Hello, owls!"

Hahahaha. I had said hello to her owls and she couldn't stop me.

Yessssss! One-nil to me!!!!!!

## Nearly kick-off

The other team were from St Pat's and quite fit boys as it happens. If you like quite fit boys.

I was just having a Midget Gem to calm me down and my back was to the road when I heard a scooter approaching. It might be the Luuurve God. I got immediate knee tremblers and jelloid knickers. But I must not expose my jelloid knickers – I must exude sophisticosity. How do you do sophisticosity without turning round?

Perhaps if I tightened my bum-oley muscles that might make for a better profile rear-wise?

No, that might look like I needed a poo.

I'll just not turn round and leave it at that.

I heard the scooter come to a halt and I said to Rosie, "What's going on?"

And she said, "It's Robbie and he's got something

hideous clinging to his back."

I looked round and Wet Lindsay was on the back of his scooter.

They got off and Robbie looked across and smiled at me. I smiled back to him. Lindsay had her head down, looking in her bag. I said to Rosie, "That bag over her head quite suits her."

What was she doing?

We watched as Robbie got his footie boots on. He is certainly in tip-top condition. It is such a waste for him to be with the Bride of Dracula. Lindsay brought out a towel and a water bottle from her bag and handed it to Robbie.

Ten seconds later

She was massaging his neck. Blimey! Has she turned into some sort of Octopussy handmaiden?

I said to the gang, "I bet she comes scampering on with the half-time oranges tucked down her bra. There is enough room... She's probably got a packed lunch in there."

Which is a fact. Surely Robbie must know about her false basooma fiasco?

Erlack! I have accidentally got parts of Wet Lindsay in my brain.

I feel dirty. It was nearly kick-off time. I was behind the tree looking over at the lads and noticed that Dave the Laugh was still missing.

"I wonder where Dave the Laugh is?"

And a voice behind me said, "Why? Are you longing for the Hornmeister, you naughty Kittykat?"

I looked round and there he was, lurking like a lurker and looking very cool in his black training stuff. He was twinkly round the eyes and said to the gang, "The vati has arrived. Now we can groove."

Ellen's head practically dropped off with redness. She still luuurves him even though she is going out with Declan.

Dave said, "Well, I'd love to stay swapping make-up hints with you girls, but there are arses to kick."

As he was going by me, I said, "Erm... Dave, would you give me a call? I want to ask you something."

He looked at me. "If you are hoping to entice me into *rummachen unterhalb der Taille*, I have told you before, you are embarrassing yourself."

Ooooohhhhh, he is sooo annoying.

The lads were yelling at him, "Oy, Dave, get a wriggle on, mate!!"

Dave started humming the theme from *Match of the Day* and jogging off backwards, waving at us. Then he turned towards the team and started doing run run leap like a mad gazelle. When he was a few metres from them, he did slow-motion running with his arms outstretched and his team started doing the same towards him. When they reached each other, they had a minor ruck.

Boys never cease to amaze me, never.

I wonder if he will phone me though? Masimo hasn't turned up. Perhaps he already has a new girlfriend.

Half time

Dave's team are winning one-nil. I'd like to say it is down to superior skill, but largely it's because Sven fell on to the St Pat's goalkeeper and the ball went over the line. St Pat's protested, but it's pointless arguing with Sven. He took the player who was arguing with him and lifted him off his feet and kissed him on the mouth.

The bloke was nearly sick, but he shut up and the goal counted.

Wet Lindsay did have half-time oranges.

Sadly not down her bra.

But even so, half-time oranges. How crap is that? Vair vair crap.

### Three minutes later

I went and stood really near to Jas. She *ignorez-vous*ed me. So I gave a pretendy piece of half-time chocolate to one of her owls. She snatched her owly away.

Tom was there and he said, "Oh, come on, you two. Put your handbags down. Come on, Jas, speak to Georgia."

She said, "Who?"

And went off flicking her fringe to speak to Emma, who turned up to hang around Dave. Jas has only known Emma for about a minute and a half. I do hate her. It's official.

She should be on my side in my time of neednosity.

After all I have done for her.

I said that to the Ace Gang as the second half started.

I said, "She is *ignorez-vous*ing me after all I have done for her."

Ellen dithered into life (unfortunately) and said, "Er... what, erm, what have you, erm, done like, for her?"

Where to begin?

I said, "For a start, I have put up with her stupid fringe-flicking for about a million years."

But it was pointless trying to get anyone's attention because they were all acting like divs in front of their boyfriends.

**5:15 p.m.**

I thought I might have to do the Heimlich manoeuvre on Ellen when Declan asked her to the cinema at the end of the match. Well, actually, I say "asked", but what happened is that he nodded his head at her and she trotted over to him like puppy dog girl. It was like a horrible love fest at the end.

I would have more pridenosity with my boyfriend. If I had a boyfriend.

**6:00 p.m.**

All alone at home.

Phone rang. I nervously picked it up, but it was only Mum telling me that they are at Grandvati's for tea and did I want to go over. Is she mad?

**6:02 p.m.**

The rest of the gang have gone to the cinema. With their

boyfriends. Not even a thought for my tragicosity. Well, to be fair, they did ask me to go, but I would have just been goosegog girl among the snoggers.

6:15 p.m.
Angus seems to understand what I am going through. He has leaped up on to my lap.

Nice.

Aaaah. He's purring.

Really loudly actually.

Nice though.

All comfy and warmy.

One minute later
Now he's snuggling into me.

Nice.

He's all cosy on my knee and I can read my *Vogue*.

One minute later
He's snuggling into my chest now, which is nice, but a bit difficult for me to move my arms.

But he's all comfy and...

Now he's on my shoulders, like a fur cape.

He's settled down now – that's nice. He's doing his snuggling and purring.

**One minute later**

Now he's back on my lap... he's actually on my magazine now.

**One minute later**

Now he's back on my chest.

I CAN'T STAND ANY MORE OF THIS!!!!!!

**Five minutes later**

It's no use him just staring at me through the window. I'm not letting him in.

**Three minutes later**

Staring and staring.

I'm going into the kitchen to see if there is anything to stave off scurvy.

**Two minutes later**

Now he's staring in through the kitchen window.

**6:30 p.m.**

He can't stare at me in the bathroom because there is frosted glass. Hahahahaha.

He'd better not burrow in through the sewage system and pop up out of the loo.

No calls from anyone.

Not Masimo, not Dave the Laugh.

Too busy with his girlfriend I suppose.

Really, I'm too upset and tired to do my beauty routine, but as someone once said, possibly on *Big Brother*, "When the going gets tough, the tough get moisturising and plucking."

If I am once again going to be spinster of the parish, I will at least be smoothy smooth.

### In the bathroom

What does Dad do with his razors? They are so blunt! I've torn my legs to ribbons. I look like I've been playing hockey with the Piranha family. Ouchy ouch ouch!!!

And ouch.

I must staunch the flow. I've probably lost an armful of blood already.

Phone rang

Oh my giddy god's pyjamas. I hobbled over with my legs covered in bits of loo paper and picked up the receiver. I tried for a casual, nonchalant sort of voice, one that didn't sound like I was bleeding to death.

"Hello."

"Hello, you cheeky Fräulein. You know you love it."

It was Dave. Oh, I felt so happy I wanted to cry.

He said, "So what's up, Kittykat?"

And I started.

"After you went on Saturday night, the Luuurve God got on his huffmobile."

Dave said, "And he didn't say anything?"

"No, he just looked at me all sort of sad."

"Was he crying?"

"Er no."

"Probably worried his mascara would run."

"Dave."

"I'm just being jovial Dave the Biscuit to lighten the mood."

"Well, don't be. I'm too upset."

"Look, Georgia, this is a bit tricky for me. There's Emma and well..."

"Well what? I'm only asking you to be like the Hornmeister and tell me what to do."

There was a pause and then he said, "OK, here's what we'll do. I'll casually bump into him..."

"And not mention pants or anything."

"No, I will leave pants out of it. I'll just say that there is nothing going on to have a girlie tizz about and..."

"You won't actually say the girlie tizz thing, will you?"

"Right, er well, I'll say... well, I don't know exactly what I will say, just that we were having a laugh because... that's what mates do."

"And that's true, isn't it?"

There was another little pause and then Dave said, "Yeah, well, listen, I have to go now."

And he was gone.

Had that gone well?

If so, why did I feel so funny?


10:30 p.m.

No call from Masimo.

**10:32 p.m.**

Still, on the bright side, we've got a budgie.

**10:40 p.m.**

Not for long I suspect. Angus and Gordy have been staring at it since Vati brought it home from the birdy sanctuary.

**Midnight**

If anyone can fix it, it's the Hornmeister. I must get the Luuurve God back. It means everything to me.

I hadn't even been able to properly show off that I was his girlfriend before I was maybe dumped.

# Elepoon in your nick-nacks

## Monday September 19th

Woke up from a dream where Dave had come up to me and said, "I didn't even mention pants and he went ballisticisimus."

And Dave had a pair of pants on his head.

And they weren't small.

### 8:15 a.m.

A bit earlier than usual. I want to make sure Jas doesn't get to Stalag 14 without me.

I want to know how Jazzy Spazzy is going to carry on her campaign of *ignorez-vous*ing me when I refuse to be *ignorez-vous*ed.

 37

**8:25 a.m.**

Thar she blows! She senses I am here and she is putting a bit of speed on.

**8:29 a.m.**

Aaaah, I have got her in my sights. Her bottom is waggling away only just in front of me. I am going to do my world-renowned speedwalking.

**8:32 a.m.**

My nose is practically on the back of her beret.

She is still pretending I am invisible girlie, but she must be able to hear me panting.

I pulled out a Jammy Dodger and held it in front of her face. She loves a Jammy Dodger.

**8:35 a.m.**

Even when I ate the Jammy Dodger walking backwards in front of her she didn't slow down.

OK, I am going in.

I leaped on her unexpectedly and pulled her beret right down over her eyes. But even then she kept marching on like nothing had happened. It was only when she crashed into the postman, who was bending over filling his sack, that she had to stop and take her beret off.

The postman went bonkers and shouted at her to "stop playing silly beggars!!!!".

I have said this before and I will say it again, how come anyone who puts a badge on goes immediately insane?

And anyway, why do they need a badge?

A badge that says "postman" or "caretaker".

Don't they know who they are?

I took advantage of the brouhaha and stepped in front of Jas. Eyeball to eyeball.

I said, "Jazzy, it's me, your old pally."

She was all red and her fringe looked like a tumble-dried ferret.

She said, "I know it's you. I know it's you because every time anything bad happens or someone is shouting, you'll be around."

I said, "That's not fair. What about the time I helped you get off with Hunky by pretending that you were normal and popular?"

She shrugged and said, "Yeah, well..."

"And remember the puffball skirt incident?"

That got her.

She said, "It looked nice."

"Wrong, Jas. You looked like you had a little elepoon in your nick-nacks, didn't you?"

She shrugged, but she knew I was right really because Astonishingly Dim Monica had worn a puffball skirt to the school play and Rosie started singing, "Nellie the elephant packed her PANTS and said goodbye to the circus"!!

I had her on the ropes now and said, "Come on, little pally, think of all the larfs we've had. Come on, I need you... I need you because you are so vair vair wise. You are tip-top to the toppimost full of wisdomosity... and I am a fool."

Jas was flicking her stupid fringe, but I didn't strike her. She said, "You bring it on yourself."

I put my arm round her and held her arm down so she would stop the fringe-fiddling business. I said, "I know, Jazzy, but that is because I am full of *je ne sais quoi*."

### Stalag 14

At least Jas and me are besties again. Hurrah!

Well, until she begins to annoy me again. In about a minute.

**RE**

What is it with Miss Wilson? She's obsessed with rudey-dudeyness. Since the camping trip when she, I think deliberately, exposed herself to Herr Kamyer in the shower, she's gone sex mad.

I said to Rosie, "Is she wearing lippy? Or has she just eaten a strawberry Mivvy?"

Rosie was making a little beard for her pencil case so she was a bit "busy", but she took the trouble to look up and said, "Most people wear lippy on their lips, not on their nostrils and chin. But at least she is giving it a go."

I wish she wasn't "giving it a go".

We were having to discuss the Song of Songs from the Bible. It's about some old ancient bloke who was a king and a ye olde handmaiden-type person. I think it's mostly about snogging, but not as we know it. I said to Jools, "What does 'he put his hand on my lock' mean when it's at home?"

Jools said, "Ask her."

I had nothing else to do, and Miss Wilson would go boring on if I didn't interrupt her. And I had done all I could to pass the time, even my toenails, sooo...

I put my hand up. Well, actually, I put them both up as a sort of novelty. Like an orang-utan.

I said, "Miss Wilson, if we translated ye olde Bible into modern language – you know, that made sense – well, what number on the Snogging Scale would 'he put his hand on my lock' be?"

Miss Wilson went sensationally red, nearly as red as her nostrils and chin.

"Well, Georgia, erm, yes, that is interesting... yes, making a connection between biblical love and rituals and so forth, and, erm, modern vocabulary, erm..."

Rosie put aside her beard because we sensed a comedy opportunity. We all stared at Miss Wilson's bob.

We were not disappointed. The bob was in full bob.

German

It's not often that we get two comedy opportunities for the price of one, but happy days here we are.

Herr Kamyer had hardly had time to adjust his knitted tie before Rosie started.

She said, "Herr Kamyer, we have just had a *sehr* interesting talk with Miss Wilson."

Herr Kamyer was blinking through his glasses in a kindly and interested way. It's tragic really. He said, "Oh *ja*?"

Rosie said, "*Ja*, it is *sehr sehr* interesting. It was from the Bible. In der German Bible *vas ist*..."

Herr Kamyer said, "Der word *für* Bible in German is..."

Rosie said, "Vat ever. In der German Bible *vas ist der* translation *für* 'he put his handchen on my lock'?"

Herr Kamyer looked like a goldfish in a knitted tie. He said, "I'm afraid I do not know dis expression."

I said, "It is int der Bible, Herr Kamyer, int der Song of Songen. It ist about der *Knutschen*!"

Rosie was in her own German snogging world by now.

She said, "Would it be *Abscheidskuss*?"

I said, "Or perhaps *AUF GANZE GEHEN*!!!!!!!"

**4:30 p.m.**

Walking home with the gang.

Funnily enough, I sort of forgot about the Luuurve God for a while. But after the others had gone I felt really miz.

I let myself in to my "home".

No one in.

Do you know, Jas even knows what she is going to have for supper most nights.

More to the point, she GETS some supper.

Still, as long as my mum can waggle her enormous basoomas around in the swimming pool with her mates.

That's what counts.

### Two minutes later
Had a bowl of Shreddies. The milk was past its sell-by date so with my luck I'll get milkytosis. Which will make my nostrils flare up to twice their size, and I will start eating grass.

### In the front room
Libby, my charming but insane little sister, has christened the budgie Bum-ty.

Bum-ty doesn't look very chirpy.

Who would with two cats staring at you.

Have they been there all day?

### 5:30 p.m.
Ooooh, I am so vair bored. And depressed at the same time.

**6:00 p.m.**

The Family Mad have come in.

And Uncle Eddie is here. Hurray!!!

They caught me by surprise so I couldn't barricade myself in my room.

Uncle Eddie larged in first.

He said, "I've got one for you. Two nuns driving along at night on a lonely forest road and a vampire leaps out and on to the bonnet. The nun who's driving says to the other nun, 'Quick, show him your cross!' and the second nun shouts, 'Get off the bloody bonnet!'!!!!!"

And he went wheezing and cackling off into the kitchen.

Grown women pay money to see him taking his clothes off to music.

I don't know what to say.

Yes I do.

I would pay him not to take his clothes off.

In fact, I might go along one night to one of his baldyman gigs and shout, "Get 'em on!!!"

No. I won't do that.

I may as well go and get my jimjams on. When you are visiting the cakeshop of agony, they don't mind what you

♡ 45

wear in there. Most of their customers are in their jimjams. With big swollen eyes. And covered in dribble.

God, I am really depressed now.


### In the lounge in my jimjams

Vati came in with a pork pie. Taking his health seriously then.

He said, "What's the matter with you?"

Not that he cares.

I said, "I'm depressed actually."

He said, "Depressed, at your age? You'll be saying you're bored next."

"That is what I was going to say next."

Vati looked at me and sat down. He patted my knee with his pork-pie-free hand.

Oh dear God, he had touched my jimjams.

He said, "Do you know what my mum used to say when I was bored?"

Oh, this would be good. It was bound to be something to do with making hats out of eggboxes.

I was about to say, "I'm bored enough as it is without you telling me about prehistoric hats."

But he was rambling on.

"She used to say, 'I'll. tell you what... bang your head against a wall and that will take your mind off it.'"

Charming.

In bed

7:00 p.m.

I can hear Libby trying to teach Bum-ty the words to "Dancing Bean".

I think Bum-ty might not be long for this world. He's got two cats staring at him night and day and now a mad toddler is shoving a sausage through the cage and singing.

Three pairs of mad eyes looking at you.

7:30 p.m.

Was that a scooter coming near?

7:32 p.m.

No.

Oh, good. Now I'm having hallucinations.

Of the earhole.

Ear-lucinations.

**7:35 p.m.**

No.

Oh yes.

Oh my God.

It IS a scooter coming up the road.

I looked through the window.

It was Masimo!!!!

Oh *merde*.

I hadn't got time to do anything.

I was in my jimjams.

I had plaited all my hair because I was so bored and depressed.

I ran down to the front room and said, "Mum, quick, I need you."

For once, Mum did what I asked her.

I told her to tell Masimo that I was out.

As the scooter came to a halt outside, I was scarpering up the stairs and I whispered to her, "Don't start a conversation with him, will you? Don't tell him about yourself."

She said, "Don't make me change my mind."

And at the top of the stairs I said, "Don't let him see Dad in his leisure trousers. Please."

Then the doorbell rang.

I bobbed down and looked through the banisters. I could only see the bottom bit of the open door.

I heard Masimo's voice. He said, "*Ciao.*"

I had thought I might never hear "*ciao*" again. Oh, what was he here for???

Mum said, "Masimo, what a lovely surprise. You look, er... lovely."

Oh nooooo, she was talking to him like he was a boy and she was a girl! Did she have her cardigan buttoned up? I couldn't remember...

Masimo said, "Er, I have come, *scusi* for my English, I have come for to give Georgia..."

Mum interrupted. "I'm afraid she had to stay late for, erm, hockey."

Masimo said, "Ah yes, she is good for hockey, I think... but I come for to give her... a letter. *Grazie mille.*"

And he was gone.

I crouched down by my window and looked out. Masimo accelerated away down the street. He was wearing a leather coat. My heart skipped a beat to see him.

In a way, I didn't want to go down and get the letter.

What if it said, "*Ciao, bella...* you are... how you say in English... dumped."

Mum came rushing up to my room.

She handed me the letter and said, "What does it say?"

I said, "It says, 'What fine weather we are having for this time of year...' Mum, I DON'T KNOW what it says because I haven't opened it yet. I am waiting to open it privately. Do you see?"

She slammed out of the room saying, "Sorry for being interested in your life."

I daren't read it.

Five minutes later

I've tried to psychically feel what it might say.

It's not very nice to dump someone by post, is it?

Just because they had a bit of a twist with Dave the Whatsit.

Two minutes later

Ripped it open.

Three minutes later

Well, the nub and the gist is...

I think...

That Masimo says he thinks that he was a bit out of order. And that Dave had been to see him and said that we were just mates having a laugh.

But (and this is the worrying bit) Masimo said he thought that maybe I wanted just to have fun with my mates. And that maybe I am too young for a relationship with him.

He doesn't know.

He is thinking.

He wants me to think too.

And that we can meet at the Stiff Dylans gig on Saturday, and then we will talk.

He just signed it "Masimo".

No kisses.

Not a "I am missing you and want to snog you within an inch of your life."

Hmmm. So am I semi-dumped?

Fifteen minutes later

The one person I would like to talk to about this is the Hornmeister.

But I can't.

I had to make do with Jazzy Spazzy.

### Phoned Jas

I told her about the note.

"I think what the note means is that I have got another chance. To show that I want to be with him. And that I am not a twisting fool. I am, in fact, a sophisticate wise beyond my years. And so on."

She just went, "Hmmmmm."

"He is, in fact, asking me to reveal my inner maturiosity, of which I have got bloody bucketfuls as it happens. And he is requesting me to put away my inner fool. That is what I think."

"Hmmmmmmmmmmmm."

What does she mean, "Hmmmmmmmmmmm"?

### Midnight

"Hmmmmmmmmmmmm" does not mean "Yes yes, I agree with you."

It means "Hmmmmmmmmmmmm".

Anyway she can "hmmmm" away. I am going to start my campaign of maturiosity tomorrow.

# FIRE!!! I'm gonna teach you to burn!

## Tuesday September 20th
Stalag 14
Break

It's bloody nippy noodles outside.

Mabs said, "Shall we work out a new disco inferno dance for Saturday's gig? To warm us up?"

I said, "Er, well, it's a bit soon after our last triumph, don't you think?"

Rosie said, "No. A triumph is not a triumph until you have gone too far."

Jas said, "I'm freezing."

To change the subject away from mad dancing, that I am now eschewing with a firm hand, I said, "Well, Jas, we are all freezing. Why don't you use some of your very well-known forest skills and start a lovely campfire? I bet you've got your special fire-making stick in your rucky, haven't you?"

Jas said, "Don't be silly."

I said, "I'm not being silly. I'm being frozen to within an inch of my life. Anyway, you can't do it without Hunky, can you? You're frightened of fire."

"I am not frightened of fire."

"Yes you are."

"No I'm not."

"Look at me, Jas. I'm a flame and I'm coming near your fringe."

And I started doing an ad-hoc flame improv, wiggling my body and making my arms all snakey, touching Jas's fringe and making a *whooshing* noise.

Jas was getting quite red and there was deffo a touch of tomato about her ears.

Rosie, Jools and the rest of the gang started snaking and shaking about, going "*Whoosh whoosh*".

Jas finally lost her rag and said, "I can make a fire! Go and get some twigs and I'll show you."

Excellent!

Ten minutes later

Brillopads.

Jas actually did it. She rubbed her special little fire-making stick in a wedge thing. She did happen to have her special "rubbing sticks" with her in her haversack. I don't know why, but I knew she would have. She is very secretive about her rucky. I bet she has several changes of different type weight pants in there. And possibly a collection of molluscs. We may never know. At least, I may never know because I will never be putting my hand in there. My hand will never be upon her lock and that is a fact!!!

Anyway, it was really jolly sitting round our little campfire. It was made mostly out of crisp packets. To be fair, there was more smoke than flame, but we pretended we were really really warmey warm. I said, "Shall we sing the old traditional campfire song, little Ace Gang pallies?"

And they all went, "Yeah!!!"

And I said, "What is it?"

Then I remembered some old crap recording of *Top of the Pops* in the 70s that my dad had. I'd shown it to the gang. I said, "Let's sing 'Fire' by that bloke who wore a helmet that was actually on fire. And when he sang on *Top of the Pops*, his helmet set fire to the ceiling. By the way, Ro Ro, do NOT mention that to Sven. He's bound to want to do it and then it's goodbye to any club that we go to."

Anyway, where was I? Oh yes, we were just sitting round our campfire singing, "FIRE!!! I'm going to teach you to burn. FIRE! I'm gonna teach you to learn!!!" when out of nowhere came Wet Lindsay. The octopus in the ointment. With her assistant fascist, ADM. She saw us round our innocent "campfire" and went absolutely ballisticisimus.

She was yelling, "You absolute twits!!!!! Step away, step away!!! Monica, get Mr Attwood and tell him there is a fire in the fives court..."

Twenty minutes later

What a fuss and a kerfuffle.

Mr Attwood practically pooed himself with delight. He's been standing by with flame retardant since *MacUseless* when somebody accidentally set fire to Nauseating P. Green. The fact that the "inferno" had gone out by the time he got there didn't stop him. He came leaping up and made us stand and watch from "a safe distance" (the edge of the fives court) while he donned his special breathing apparatus. He was shouting through the mask, "There may be toxic fumes."

I was yelling, "It's out, Mr Attwood!"

But he couldn't hear me.

He squirted his extinguisher thing until there was foam up to the top of his welligogs. Quite, quite extraordinarily bonkers.

### Three minutes later

He took off his mask and looked at the huge pile of foam.

He said, "I've made the area safe – I'll just radio in to Headquarters to say I've achieved a result safety-wise and no casualties."

From his "fire sack" he fished out an enormous walkie-talkie thing.

Wet Lindsay said, "Right, you lot, the headmistress's office. NOW!"

Oh no, not Slim.

She frogmarched us off, chuntering on to ADM and giving me the evils every now and again. She just absolutely loves it times a million.

If she can upset me, she's made up.

Jas said, "Oh, now I'll never get to be a prefect. This is all your fault, Georgia. Again."

I said, "Er, I think you are the firestarter, crazy firestarter Jas."

Rosie said, "Do you think Slim will beat us to death with her chins?"

As we sloped along at one mile an hour, we could hear Mr Attwood shouted into his walkie-talkie. "Z Victor 1 to B.D. Are you receiving me? Over."

Astonishingly barmy.

Jools said, "Who is he talking to?"

And I said, "He's talking to Headquarters. And you know who that is, don't you?"

Ellen said, "No, I... er... is it... erm, is it, like... Headquarters or something?"

We just looked at her.

I said, "He is talking to the radio in his shed. And do you know who is listening? No one."

I asked "permission" to go to the piddly-diddly department and Wet Lindsay came with me. Like I was going to escape through the loo window! Actually, I did do that once, but that is not the point. As I was in the cubicle, trying not to make any piddly-diddly noises because I didn't want her to hear me, she said, "You really are the most appalling little tart, Georgia Nicolson. Robbie did the right thing dumping you and Masimo must be dying to get rid of you."

I started to say, "Actually, I think boys like girls with foreheads…"

But she said, "Nicolson, if you don't want to spend the rest of the term recovering from a very bad hockey injury, I advise you to SHUT UP right now."

As I walked back under armed guard, I thought, how could Robbie kiss her?

Erlack.

I think he must have clinical depression after I stopped going out with him. When she had been yelling at me, I could see right up her nostrils. Also she didn't have mascara on and her eyelashes were like albino mouse eyelashes. No, they weren't as nice as that; they were like duck eyelashes. And ducks don't have eyelashes.

I hate her times a million. When I get over enticing Masimo back into my web of luuurve, I will concentrate on ruining her life and saving Robbie.

Outside Slim's office

Three minutes later

The Little Titches, also known as the Dave the Laugh fanclub, were in the outer torture chamber with the Ace Gang when I got there. Wet Lindsay went off to get Elvis.

I said, "Hello, Titches, what are you up for? GBH? Titchiness?"

Ginger Titch said, "We were making up a tribute to Dave the Laugh in the loos."

And I said, "Where is the crime in that?"

And the littlest one said, "We broke the loo seat with our stamping."

"There is no justice in this place. It squashes any sign of creativitosity."

The Little Titches nodded. Ginger said, "Miss, do you like Dave the Laugh the bestiest? We do."

All of the gang looked at me and I went a bit red.

Jas said, "Yes, do you "accidentally" like Dave the Laugh, Georgia?"

Ellen was looking and blinking and started saying, "Why would... I mean, what... Dave and... well, what is that..."

Rosie started shouting "FIRE!! I'm gonna teach you to burn, FIRE!!" and doing *whooshing* and flame dancing when Slim opened her door suddenly and said, "I'm glad that you are all in such a jolly mood. Let's see if we can change that. You two first-formers in my room, now."

The two Little Titches started to follow her. After her gigantic bottom had waddled off, they got to her door and looked round. I saluted them by putting my finger on my nose and making it stick up like a piggie.

They saluted back and even did a little grunt.

They are top girls for Little Titches.

Five minutes later

We could hear muffled shouting and then a bit of crying.

Rosie said, "She is beating them with her chins."

God, if Slim was going to go ballistic over a loo seat, we were deffo going to get a severe mental thrashing.

Then Wet Lindsay arrived, accompanied by Mr Attwood. In a wheelchair. What????

Was he too lazy even to walk across the playground?

A man in his physical condition should not be in charge of the safety of high-spirited youth.

Or any people.

Or anything.

Wet Lindsay looked at me like I was snot in a skirt. It turned out that Elvis had slipped in his own foam and done his back in. I bet he hasn't.

He was moaning on for England, as usual.

"How am I supposed to do my job now?"

I was going to say, "Oh, you know, the usual way, sitting perving in your hut."

But I didn't.

He was rambling on.

"You have no thought for others. When I was a boy, we had respect for our elders."

Moan moan. Here we go. It will be, "In my day we used to enjoy ourselves just by picking our own noses."

I said, "Well, as it happens, Elvis, er, I mean Mr Attwood, I agree with you. You are clearly too old to be working. It's cruel. In fact, I am going to have a word with our headmistress and suggest she gives you the big goodbye you so richly deserve."

Wet Lindsay had her usual spazerama attack.

She said, "Shut up and grow up!"

Charming.

### Slim's office

Oh, I am soooo bored with being told off. It is giving me the megadroop. I should be at home glamming myself up for the Luuurve God and practising my new sophisticosity. Just in case he forgives me. Instead of which I am in an office counting chins.

Slim was completely jelloid. In fact, her whole body was having a chin-a-thon. Of course, it was me who got it in the neck. As if I started the bloody fire. I just did a bit of *whooshing*.

Slim said, "It's always you, isn't it, Georgia? What happened this time? Is it another miscarriage of justice?"

Well, at least she was being reasonable for once.

I said, "Well actually, Miss, yes it is. You see it was minus 50 outside and we were terribly cold, so J... I mean we, decided to use our woodland skills that we learned on our magnificent camping trip with Herr Kamyer and..."

Slim looked at me.

"You mean you set fire to some rubbish in the fives court."

I said, "Well, that's one way of putting it."

Mr Attwood lurched to life.

"I'm in agony, Headmistress, because of an act of senseless arson. By arsonists."

I don't know what it is about the word arse-onists, but it does give me the inward hysteria. Mr Attwood had more or less said "arse" in front of Slim. I daren't look at Rosie.

Slim looked at me.

"It's always you, Georgia. Why can't you grow up?"

I nearly said, "I'm growing as fast as I can. Look at the size of my nungas!"

Wet Lindsay had to put her oar in.

"The trouble is, of course, that she does lead the others into it."

Oh yeah, that'll be the day.

I started to say, "Well actually, funnily enough, this time it was..."

And Jas looked at me like an annoying fringey puppy. Dear God, she actually did want to be a prefect. It is vair nice of me to even be mates with her under the circs.

It's an act of charity really. And when I had mentioned my plan for sophisticosity she had said, "Hmmmmmmmmm mmmm."

But then she looked at me again. A bit tearful. Oh, bloody hell.

It had to be done.

I said, "Oh, OK, yes, it was my idea..."

Rosie and Jools said, "Well, not really. We all..."

But I ploughed on.

"Whatever they say, they are my mates and they are covering for me. It was my idea, but it was only a tiddly tiny firey thing."

Mr Attwood said, "I bet that's what the baker said about the fire he started that turned into the Great Fire of London."

What is he rambling on about? We're not even in London.

Anyway, the long and the long of it is that the others have got a ticking-off and reprimands and I have got detention...

and worst of all... have to "help" Mr Attwood this term. Again.

Oh, what larks we'll have.

Not.

### Detention
### 4:00 p.m.

Jas squeezed my arm as she left for home and pressed a secret stash of Midget Gems into my hand. She said, "You are truly my bezzie mate of all time, Georgia."

And she is not wrong. I am without doubtosity top mate of all time.

### 4:05 p.m.

Luckily, I have got Miss Wilson as my prison guard so I will be able to make best possible use of my time.

First of all, I am going to plan my Luuurve God re-entrancing plan.

### Fifteen minutes later

The Luuurve God re-entrancing plan.

1. "You are never alone with your lippy and mascara." I am going to make a sort of pouch that fits under my bra and pants so that I have a secret supply at all times. Even if the Luuurve God pops up unexpectedly (oo-er) I can refresh by reaching for my pouch.

NB. Make my pouch out of nice softy soft material so that I can wear it in bed. In case the Luuurve God pops up unexpectedly in the night. (Oo-er.)

2. I will exude sophisticosity with just a hint of glaciosity. I think the European Luuurve God likes this sort of thing. He is not, after all, a crude Viking like Sven who quite frankly wouldn't recognise glaciosity if it hit him in the face. On the contrary, Sven would think you were playing hard to get because you were a lezzie and that would give him the Horn.

Four minutes later

3. Be nice. This means regrettably I will not be disco dancing like a tit any more. When the Stiff Dylans play, I will waft around like a... wafting thing on waft

♡ 67

tablets. I will laugh lightly, but at no time don a false beard.

False beards are over. I will never wear the beard again.

Ditto horns.

And finally...

4. I will not do arm-wrestling or any kind of wrestling with Dave the Laugh.

Dave the Laugh is no longer a laugh to me. He is Emma's boyfriend and my mate.

Actually, I wonder where he is? I haven't seen him for yonks. Ah, well. Stop thinking about Dave the Laugh. He is not in this re-entrancing document.


Five minutes later

Blimey, I have finished my manifesto and it is still not time to go home. Miss Wilson is humming and reading something. It had better not be some humming idea she has for the school play. I am not doing a humming version of *Rom and Jule* and that is a fact. I am not humming in tights.

## Four minutes later

I know what I will do next. I will make another scale for the Ace Gang. On how they too can become great mates like what I am.

## Ten minutes later

Great mates scale.

1. Offer a mate a Midget Gem without being asked.
2. Share your last Jammy Dodger even though you really want it and your mate may be flicking her fringe about.
3. Listen to your mate rambling on about themselves when you have got vair important things to do yourself (e.g. nails, plucking etc.).
4. Be with your mate through thick and thin. Or even if they are both thick and thin. Tee-hee. I made a great mate-type joke there. Did you see??? Which leads me to Number 5.
5. Always be game for a laugh even though you may be blubbing on the inside.

Crikey, I am coming out of this scale VAIR well indeed. But as everyone knows, I do not blow my own trumpet. I just blow my own HOOOOORN.

No, I don't. And that brings me to my tip-toppy of the toppimost great mate scale.

6. Even when they have all the reason in the universe to be top dog (i.e. when they are the girlfriend of a Luuurve God, even if it is slightly on a sale-or-return basis) a top mate does not blow their own trumpet. Or snitch on her less fortunate mates.

**6:00 p.m.**
On my way home at last. Miss Wilson said, "Well, now that's over, I expect you are excited about our workshop for *Romeo and Juliet*."

Oh no, the humming in tights.

Miss Wilson was rambling on.

"I've been busy coming up with some original ideas. I think it's important to keep up with you modern girls. I hope we can make this a... erm... groovy production."

Oh dear God.

I was walking along as fast as I could out of the school gates. She is wearing a knitted hat. It has a bobble on it.

That is all I am saying. I am not being bobble-ist.

She turned left out of the gate with me. Please, please let her not be going my way. I had done my detention!!!

She was still going on.

What if she linked arms with me?????

"I know you girls might think that us teachers are not very, you know... hip."

What? She was trying to be my mate! Please don't let her tell me about her growing feelings for Herr Kamyer. Maybe she'll call him by his first name. I don't even know what that is. I don't want to know. I bet it's Rudi!!!! Stop being my friend!! I've got enough on my plate without having to be friends with knitted people.

She didn't hear my inner screaming though. She said, "Yes, I think you will see that I do listen to your ideas and so on. For instance, when Jas suggested that perhaps Juliet could have a little companion – a sort of puppet dog – I thought 'Bingo'!!"

I couldn't stop myself, even though I had taken a vow of silence until she shut up or I died. I said, "Er, Miss Wilson, do you remember your last 'Bingo' idea? Do you remember, you said that juggling would be 'happening', but what actually 'happened' was that Melanie toppled over with the weight of her own basoomas and the oranges bounced into the audience."

Miss Wilson said, "Well, that's the excitement of theatre, isn't it? The danger, the risk!"

"Yes, my grandvati said an orange nearly took his eye out, so..."

Miss Wilson fortunately saw a bus coming and scampered off to get it. Thank the Lord.

It really is tragic how keen she is to get on with us. Touching really, if you like that sort of thing. Which I don't.

Thank goodness no one I knew saw me walking along talking to a teacher. I may just as well have gone to a leper colony if they had. Or become a policewoman.


Twenty minutes later

My road at last. Angus was round in Naomi's garden. He likes to go over to Mr and Mrs Across the Road for his evening poo.

Mr and Mrs Across the Road are vair unreasonable about

it. They say he always chooses to poo in their rare heathers windowbox. I explained to them, that is because the soil is nice and softy and he doesn't have to do any digging. But you can't tell people.

When he last came over to complain, Mr Across the Road said, "How long does his breed of cat live? Is it nearly over?"

I said with great dignitosity (I like to think), "Angus is half Scottish wildcat and sometimes he hears the call of the wild and longs to poo somewhere that reminds him of home. Hence the heather."

Mr Across the Road stomped off though. Some people don't understand the poetry of life. Or even the poo-etry of life. Hahahaha. I have just made an inward joke.

### one minute later

When Angus saw me, he did his weird croaky miaow thing. And waved his tail about. His tail is still a bit crooked from his car accident. (The accident being that the car wasn't the huge mouse on wheels that Angus thought it was.) Otherwise, he is top dog catwise.

He came bounding over, purring around my legs. Which is nice, but it makes it really difficult to walk without falling over and breaking your neck. Now he has started his pouncey game. He pretends my ankles are his prey and hides behind something until my ankles loom in view. Then he tries to kill them.

I managed to beat him off with my rucky.

Then I noticed that Oscar, Junior Blunder Boy and all-round idiot, was lurking around on his wall, pretending to talk on his phone to all his mates. A.k.a. the Blunder Boys. He was going, "Yeah, check it... for real... awwwrite."

Absolute bloody wubbish of the first water.

I'd be amazed if he can work his phone and keep his trousers up at the same time. I used to prefer him when he just played keepie-uppie for ages. Now he's taking an interest in me, if you know what I mean, and I think you do.

When he stopped pretending to talk on his phone, he shouted over to me. "Ay, girl! Do you believe in love at first sight... or am I going to have to walk by again?"

Then he flicked his fingers and said, "For real."

Good Lord.

I didn't say anything.

What is there to say?

Besides "Go away" a LOT.

As I walked in my gate, Naomi came slinking along, waggling her bottom about. She displays no glaciosity or sophisticosity. Things are very different in the cat world. If I was a pussycat, entrancing a Luuurve God, I would merely have to lie on my back and display my girlie parts to him. Or maybe lick my bum-oley area, and not only him, but every boy in the area would be following me around like fools.

Angus and Naomi slunk off together under Dad's useless clown car. Vati has got a fur driving-wheel cover now. There is absolutely no need for it. Mind you, there is no need for Dad either.

Front room
One minute later

Vati was in his recreational area, a.k.a. lying on the couch getting fatter.

He lurched into life when I tried to slope up the stairs.

He said, "Where have you been until now?"

I said, "Why? Have you been waiting to tell me how much you appreciate me as a daughter and that although you will never be seeing me again once I am twenty-one, you have liked me entertaining you through your twilight years?"

♡

"No, I bloody well didn't want to say that and stop being so bloody cheeky. Where have you been?"

"Erm, I was doing extra hockey."

"What, without your boots or kit which is thrown on the floor of your bedroom or 'rubbish tip', as I call it?"

I said, "Father, why have you been in my room? You know it is *verboten*. I may write to my MP and..."

He is sooooo violent. His slipper just missed my ponytail.

I wandered into the kitchen. Mum, Libby and Gordy were making some cakey thing. Which I will not be eating under any circumstances, including famine. Libby was covered in dough stuff. It was clinging to her raincoat and wellingtons. She came running over to me yelling, "It's bad boy, it's Gingeeeee! Kissy kiss, Ginger."

Oh gadzooks. She started climbing up my legs like a mad monkey in boots.

Oh good, now I am covered in cake mix, hurrah. Things are really looking up.

Mum said, "What did you get detention for this time?"

Why is everyone sooooo suspicious? I am not surprised I get detention all the time because no one will give me a chance. I could show her my "how to be a great mate" scale, but I won't.

I grabbed a sausagey thing from the cooker. It may have some nutritional value, you never know.

I was just going up to my room when Mum said, "Dave popped round earlier. He's a cool-looking boy, isn't he? If I was a few years younger, I wouldn't mind tangling tonsils with him."

Oh, how very disgusting.

I took the sausage/spam thing out of my mouth. I felt besmirched.

I said, "Mum, what were you wearing when he came round?"

She looked at me.

"Why? This."

I said, "What – that tiny skirt and even tinier top? I'm surprised he didn't call the prostitute police."

She snapped then.

"Don't be so bloody cheeky."

Libby joined in then. She stood with her hands on her hips and yelled, "Yes, bloody chinky."

9:00 p.m.
I wonder what Dave was going to say?

♥ 77

I wish I'd been in, instead of being a great mate. I would have really liked to see him.

And he's not bad on the great mates scale himself. He talked to the Luuurve God for me.

Maybe I should phone him. And thank him.

### One minute later

No, I can't because of my new re-entrancing a Luuurve God plan.

I am going to distract myself by making my little pouch.

### 9:15 p.m.

I am wearing my pouch. I am going to sleep in it tonight to make sure it is softy soft enough and so on. If I wake up in the night, I might feel for it (oo-er) and do a practice application.

### 9:20 p.m.

Libby is practising her snogging skills on Mr Potato Head. Surely this can't be right at her age? Shouldn't she mostly be pretending to be a fairy and playing with elves?

This is disgusting. Libby is going "mmmmmmmmm naiiice" and making lip-smacking noises.

I shouted downstairs.

"Hello, my sister Libby, also your daughter, is snogging a potato in my bed. What are you going to do about it?"

Dad started yelling uncontrollably. I wonder if he is having the male menopause? If he starts growing breasts, I will definitely be running away with the circus. Although to be fair, he would have a better chance of getting a job with them.

I could hear him going on.

"Connie, have you been using my bloody razors again? I've nearly cut my chin off."

Ah well, time for bobos.

I went back into my room and shut the door.

Libby is now doing a sort of smoochy dance with Mr Potato Head. It involves a lot of botty-wiggling.

What do they teach her at playschool? When I was little, we used to do face-painting and so on. Our tiny faces covered with little flowers and hearts. Libby wrote BUM on Josh's face in indelible marker.

I said to Bibbs, "Don't you want to take Mr Potato Head into your nice bed? In your own room. In your own lovely, snugly…"

She put her face really near mine and said, "Shhhhhhhh."

Midnight

I had to read *Heidi* to Libby and Mr Potato Head. She never tires of tales of cheese. I do.

The bit that makes her laugh the most is when the little crippled girl falls out of her wheelchair.

It's not right.

# Suddenly he got his maracas out

## Wednesday September 21st
### Assembly
### 9:00 a.m.

Oh, hurrah! We are having an "ad-hoc" assembly. No proper hymns that we can improvise hilarious lyrics to. No "Breathe on me BREAST of God" or "There are some green PANTS far away without a city wall…"

Hang on a minute though, things are looking up. On to the stage came Herr Kamyer in a check shirt and a cowboy hat. With a guitar. And he is accompanied by Miss Wilson on ukulele.

I said to Rosie, "I didn't even know she could play the ukulele."

Two minutes later
She can't.

This is torture. I don't know if you have ever heard the Country and Western version of "All things bright and beautiful", but I thoroughly don't recommend it.

I said to Rosie, "Quickly leap on stage and grab Herr Kamyer's guitar and kill him with it."

She said, "Righty-o," and started moving along the line. When she got to ADM on guard duty, she said to her, "Women's trouble" and skipped off to the loos.

Damn.

Fifty-five million years later we were set free. Well, free if you think double maths is freedom. Which it isn't.

Maths
Oh, shut up about numbers, why don't you?

Lunch
Behind the fives court. Right, this was my chance to

introduce the question of sophisticosity into the whole boynosity area.

I began, "I'd like to open this meeting of the Ace Gang..."

They were all looking at me attentively. Well, if you call people chewing and fiddling with their fringes and being fools attentive.

I went on, "I have called this meeting of the Ace Gang..."

Jools said, "One for all and all for one and one in all for one of us and so on?"

I said, "Yes, well, shall we get on?"

Ellen said, "Shall we do the group hug?"

I said, "I think we can take the group hug as done."

Mabs said, "I really like the group hug."

Oh dear *Gott in Himmel*.


Four minutes later

The group hug practically turned into a love-in. Rosie would not let me go. She knows it annoys me so she keeps doing it.

Eventually though, I beat her off and started again.

"The thing, the serious thing I want to discuss is..."

Rosie said, "My Viking wedding?"

"Well, no I..."

But it was too late. She had her beard out.

### Afternoon break

I will try again.

Mr Attwood wheeled past us, tutting. Tut away, lunatic man.

### Two minutes later

We watched while he got stuck trying to get up the ramp into the science block. Unfortunately, the Titches were passing and he harassed them into pushing him. While they were huffing and puffing, he actually opened a sandwich and started eating it.

I said to the gang, "He luuurves ligging about in that wheelchair. I bet he hasn't even got a bad back."

Rosie said, "Have you thought about being a nurse? I think you've got the hands for it."

I didn't get the chance to mention the sophisticosity question because Jas started going on about Tom. Is he going to go to college in Hamburger-a-gogo land? Blah blah blah. He wants to go visit the maybe college after Chrimboli.

Should she go with him? Blah blah blah.

What she actually said was, "Should I go with him? It's an area very rich in wildlife."

I said, "Oh well, you must go then. You can set fire to most of Texas and gather crusted newts to your heart's content. I only wish I could come. However, I have a life and maybe a boyfriend..."

Jas got into her huffmobile. Typico. Anything to do with Hunky or her fringe and she gets the hump. She was doing fringe-fiddling to the max.

I said, "Look, Jas, all I am saying is that we decided that you should let Tom ping off elastic-bandwise and then he can come pinging back. Possibly with gifts. Maybe some new owls."

"But you don't know that for sure, do you? I mean in *Rom and Jule*, Jule wakes up after pretending to commit suicide and Rom actually has committed suicide."

I looked at her.

"Jas, what has some old play got to do with it? It's a made-up story."

"It might not be."

"Well it is."

"How do you know – were you there?"

I wanted to kill her. I hate her in this mood.

"No, Jas, I wasn't there. I am not four hundred and fifty-five."

"Well then."

"Well."

This could go on for years. I decided to call a truce with old arsey pants.

"Look, Jas, Tom is not going to commit suicide, is he? He's just going to go to Hamburger-a-gogo land for two weeks. That'll be enough for him. When he sees the size of their shorts, he'll come scampering back."

"Well, maybe."

"Of course he will, and also they say 'aluuuuuuuuminum' there, don't they? He won't put up with that. Will he?"

"Well..."

"And mostly of all, he doesn't wear tights like Rom, does he?"

She didn't say anything, just went a bit red.

"Jas, whatever Tom has under his trousers is between you and him."

That did it.

It doesn't take much for her to expose her violent side. She really hurt my ankle. I'm glad that she doesn't have a sword in *Rom and Jule*. But does she have a dagger at the end? It could be a bloodbath if her fringe doesn't go right.

In the gym
Rom and Jule workshop
2:00 p.m.

The "workshop" exceeded even my very high expectations. Miss Wilson was in a sort of all-in-one "playsuit". She was tremendously excited.

We were lolling around on the mats when she started clapping her hands and waving a clipboard around wildly.

"Now then, girls, attention, please, on this very exciting day. Now, here we are. We are all in Verona. Can you hear the swish of the light summer wind in the blossom trees? The gay calls of the streetsellers?"

(Rosie started honking with laughter.) But Miss Wilson was immersing herself in the gay calls and the breeze.

"We are all young, full of life and passion. Come on, girls, let's get up and show that passion. Feel the passion. Just go

with the flow. Grab a tambourine or a drum if you like!!!
Use the whole space!!!!"

### Ten minutes later

I have rarely seen anything more alarming than Miss
Wilson being free and passionate. And keep in mind, I have
seen her in her nuddy-pants and with her soap on a rope.

She was careering around, banging her tambourine...

At one point, she got on the wall bars and threw bean
bags around.

She was yelling, "Waaaaaaaaaa Waaaaaaaaa."

Quite sensationally mad.

I said to Jools mid-leap, "Poor Rudi Kamyer has no
chance."

### Twenty minutes later

As a climactic end to the workshop, Rosie showed her
inner passion by pulling her nick-nacks down and mooning
at us.

I am aching with laughter. My ribs hurt.

Hey and guess what? When I popped to the piddly-
diddly department because I thought I might have an

accident, I saw Elvis Attwood having a sly fag. And he was walking about normally. He can walk!

## Home time
Hurrah hurrah!!!

Just walking out of Stalag 14 main building, all sweaty and shiny with our berets pulled down to our eyes for comedy effect, when we noticed that Tom and Robbie were waiting at the gates.

Hell's teeth.

Jas said, "How's my head?"

I said, "Alarmingly red. How's mine?"

She looked at me and went, "Blimey."

We had to think quickly. The boys hadn't seen us because they were chatting with a few passing girls that they knew. So we dashed off to the science block loos to do emergency repair work.

I put my head upside down under the hairdryer. My hope was that Robbie secretly liked the Coco the Clown look. Jas opted for the hair pulled back in a tight little ponytail, which frankly I think is a bit of a mistake, as it exposed her very, very red ears.

I didn't say though, because I didn't want her to have a complete tiz and to-do.

As we were doing lippy and mascara (thank goodness for my pouch), Jas said, "Anyway, why are you bothering about Robbie? Masimo is your one and only, isn't he?"

"I know, but once you have been out with someone you have to keep up appearances so that every time they see you, they think, 'Oooh, I wish I could snog her to within an inch of her life.' That is just the dating code."

"Apart from if it was Mark Big Gob."

"Please don't mention him."

"Or Whelk Boy."

"Jas, just shut up and turn your skirt up."

At the gate, I was casualosity personified until Robbie said, "Hello, Georgia."

He's a good-looking bloke. And nice with it. With very blue eyes, and a firm but tender mouth. Also he has charming snogging skills, his varying pressure technique for instance... hang on a minute, was that him or Dave the Laugh?

Robbie was looking at me. Had I said anything out loud?

I said, "Hi, Robbie, nice to see you."

90

My brain went on chatting to him, "Yeah, nice to see you, you hunky brute. Why are you with old Ms No Forehead when you could be in a triple-sided manwich with me and the Luuurve God?"

Shut up, brain. That is disgusting!!!!

Tom said, "Hi, Lindsay, all right?"

And it was Ms No Forehead herself. The Bride of Dracula... I looked down at my watch (which I haven't got) and said loudly, "Oh, is that the time? I must dash."

And I hoiked up my rucky. I said to Jas, "Are you walking?"

And she looked a bit dithery.

Hang on a minute. She wasn't choosing between walking with me or walking with the Hunky Brothers and WET LINDSAY, was she?

Oh yes she was.

Lindsay ignored me as if I was invisible girlie and said, "Jas, are you going on Saturday? Maybe we could meet up before, that's if Robbie can do without me. Can you, babe?"

And she went and kissed him on the cheek. Then she pointed to her own cheek. And sort of pouted. And he had to kiss her cheek.

Dear God.

It got worse. I was sort of mesmerised by horror.

She put on an ickle girlie voice and said, "Can ickle Lindsay go to de big club all by her lickle self?"

Christ on a bike.

It was horrific. It was like when Mr Next Door came to tell me off and he was wearing his shortie dressing gown and I could see his legs.

As I walked off – walking home without my so-called bestie – Tom called after me, "See you later, Gee."

And Robbie said, "Yeah, see you Saturday."

I noticed that Jas didn't dare say anything. I don't know why I bother being a really great mate to her. Boys are nicer than girls.

I'm going to show her my Great Mates Scale and suggest she tries being one. (A great mate, not a scale.)

### Home

Bum-ty has got a ladder. He's crouching at the top of it. I don't think he likes his ladder. I think he is up there because it makes him slightly further away from the staring cats.

He hasn't said a word and his feathers are starting to fall out. Libby has been showing him pictures of cheese.

**7:00 p.m.**

I've got German homework. I have to write about the Kochs. Hurrah!!!

When he set the homework, I said to Herr Kamyer, "Can it be about the Kochs going out? Because the little Kochs like to go out, don't they? Although the bigger Kochs prefer to stay in."

The Ace Gang had a mini larf-fest but Rudi didn't get how full of hilariosity I truly am. He just looked at me with his blinky eyes and said (seriously), "*Ja*, Georgia, zat is a *gut* idea, vy not haf ze Kochs havink a wild party???"

Which made us laugh even more.

I have said it once and I will say it again, I luuurve the Kochs and the comedy magic that is the German language.

Also, Herr Kamyer's idea of a wild party is probably a game of Scrabble with Miss Wilson where they don't keep the score.

**7:30 p.m.**

I am looking through my German slang book for inspirationosity for the Koch party.

Bottom is *arsch*. To fall arse over tit is *auf die Schnauze fallen*.

**Two minutes later**
This cannot be true. With knobs on is *mit schnickschnack*.

I think, in all honesty, the first person to make up der German language was a clown. Or alternatively, a *blodman* (berk).

**8:00 p.m.**
Looking through my window.

Aaah, there is Cross-eyed Gordy stretching out on the wall.

Now he is half sitting up, swatting at something. What is he doing?

Oh, it's a bee. He's up on his hind legs swatting at the bee. He's sort of hopping along on his hind legs swatting the bee.

**One minute later**
Angus has joined him on the wall.

He's watching Gordy hopping along swatting the bee and

he is moving his head about. Following the bee.

It's the bee dance. Hop hop, swatty swat, movey head, movey head. Super cats do the bee dance.

### One minute later

Not any more.

Angus has eaten the bee. He just leaped up and ate it.

He didn't even chew it.

### Two minutes later

Lying down on my bed, recovering from the excitement of bee dancing.

I wonder who is going to be Rom? Everyone who has tried out so far has been an utter fiasco. Miss Wilson said she might have to look outside our year. Crikey, what if she asks Rudi Kamyer to do it?

### Phone rang

Aha! This will be my so-called bestie ringing up to apologise.

Mum yelled up, "Georgia, it's for you."

I lolloped downstairs, taking my time, building up my

dignitosity. I said formally into the phone, "Yes. What is it you want to say?"

"Usually, I like you to say, 'What is it you want to say, Hornmeister' but I'll let you off because I am in a casual Devil take the hindmost mood."

Dave the Laugh! My heart skipped a little beat. I said, "Guess what? Wet Lindsay talked like an ickle girl to Robbie. It was horrific. Do boys like that sort of thing in girls?"

Dave said, "It depends on what the girls are wearing."

"What?"

"Boys are very visual."

"Er, Dave, I think you mean very stupid. Anyway, it doesn't matter what Wet Lindsay wears. It can't disguise her Octopussyness."

"Listen, Chaos Queen, how's every little thing? Is your girlfriend still stropping around, rifling through his handbag, or is it all tickety-boo?"

"Well, he wrote me a note, but I haven't seen him yet. It'll be the first time on Sat. He says we should take it easy and that maybe he overreacted a bit."

Dave said, "A bit? That's like Hitler saying 'Oooh, I just meant to go for a little walk, but then I accidentally invaded Poland.'"

"No, Dave, it isn't anything like that."

"You didn't know that Hitler invaded Poland, did you?"

"Of course I did."

"You don't know where Poland is, do you?"

"Dave, I am not a complete fool."

"Where is it then?"

"It's clearly, you know, near..."

"Yes?"

"The top bit."

Dave laughed. "You are good value, Kittykat."

I was a bit red, but at least I had avoided saying that I was sort of "on trial" maturiosity-wise with the Luuurve God...

Dave said, "So you'll be at the gig on Saturday?"

"Yes, will you be there?"

"Probs."

"Dave?"

"Yep..."

"Well, Dave, will you, can you, will you not be too funny and not talk to me and so on?"

"You want me to not talk to you and not be funny and so on?"

He sounded a bit weird.

I said, "Only until, you know, the whole thing, the whole pants and comedy twisting thing dies down."

He said, "You must really like him..."

I didn't say anything.

He said, "Listen, I have to dasharoo. S'laters." And he hung up.

I think he's miffed.

Dear God, you just get one boy off the numpty seat and another one goes and sits on it.


**10:00 p.m.**

Why do cats do this? They loll about snoozing in weird places for hours.

It's never their cat basket.

Why would anything want to have a snooze on the top of the kitchen rubbish bin?

Or the loo seat?

Or the fruit bowl?

Then, after all that snoozing all day, at 10:00 p.m. they wake up and go utterly bananas. Tearing up and down the stairs. Leaping from the sofa to the television, missing and falling down the back of it. Diving into plastic bags. Wrestling with their own feet. Then shooting up the curtains and doing ad-hoc sailors' hornpipe stuff coming down...

Why?

Where does leaping up curtains and doing the hornpipe occur in primitive cat life?

### In bed

### 10:30 p.m.

Time for snoozy snooze and Luuurve Goddy dreams.

I've almost forgotten what the Luuurve God looks like.

### Thirty seconds later

Yummy scrumboes though, I know that much.

And also, Grrrrrrrrrr.

Oh dear God, I actually said that out loud. I am growling at myself.

I have got snogging withdrawal baaaaad.

In fact, maybe I have forgotten how to snog.

Oh no. I may have lost my skills puckerwise.

I need to practise.

**10:35 p.m.**

I have done something so disgusting and weird that even I am ashamed of myself.

**One minute later**

This may be another thing I will not be mentioning this side of the grave.

**One minute later**

I hope that God and Baby Jesus were momentarily looking aside. Like I am sure they do when you are having a poo.

Or when Uncle Eddie does his baldy-o-gram.

**One minute later**

I can't get the thing that I will never talk about ever again out of my brain.

**One minute later**

I can't stand this. OK, I admit it!!!!

I looked at Mr Potato Head and considered practising puckering up on him.

There you are – it's out now.

**One minute later**

Yes, I momentarily thought about snogging my little sister's cast-off.

**One minute later**

I wonder where snogging a root vegetable would come on the Snogging Scale?

Minus 50 I should think.

I bet Jas snogs her owls.

**11:00 p.m.**

I hope Dave is just having a minor hump. We are, after all, mates.

Yeah, that will be it. He will just be having a No. 7 (walking on ahead, metaphorically).

It won't be the full Humpty Dumpty.

So that's all right.

**2:00 a.m.**

Woke up from a dream that I was at a fancy-dress party. I was painted purple and in the nuddy-pants because I had gone as a jelly baby. Then Dave the Laugh came by really slowly with a girl on his back. I said, "What have you come as?"

And he said, "A tortoise."

I said, "Who's the girl on your back?"

And he said, "That's Michelle... Do you get it – mechelle?"

And he was laughing and laughing. But not in a nice way.

## Friday September 23rd
8:15 a.m.

I really need some new shoes for Saturday night. Maybe my vati is in a sunny, Devil take the hindmost sort of mood about money this morning.

I said, "Dad... I couldn't help noticing how... er... shiny, your car is. You do keep it lovely."

"No."

"Dad, I..."

"Goodbye."

I can't believe it.

Mum came mumming in, in her knickers. Well, if you can call them that.

Hang on a minute.

102

I said, "Mum, are you wearing a thong?"

She is. She is wearing a thong!

I said to her, "If you have a road accident, I will not be coming to explain your underwear to the emergency services."

She just looked at me and went off into the bathroom... Well. Then I remembered my new shoes.

I shouted to her, "Mum, could I just borrow..."

Before I could finish, she shouted back. "No."

What is the point of parents? They wonder why the youth of today goes wrong. If they would merely give us what we wanted and keep away from us, all would be well...

Instead of Mum just lending me her black Chanel stilettos and everything being nice and easy, I am now going to have to sneak into her wardrobe, smuggle them out in my bag, wear them, sneak back into her room and replace them.

They force us into a life of crime.

8:30 a.m.

On the way to school

Jas needn't think I have forgotten about her blatant lack of best mateyness. And her creepy-crawly pants behaviour around Wet Lindsay.

I am going to have the hump with her for once and see how she likes that. I am going to avoid her house and go a different way. That will teach her that you can't... she is sitting on my gate.

Damn. I hadn't even had a chance to get in my huffmobile.

She hopped off the gate and said, "Gee, I'm really sorry about last night. I couldn't sort of get out of it because of Tom and Robbie. It's not Lindsay, but the boys are brothers and... well, you know... blood is thicker than not having a forehead."

I went, "Hmmph."

She got her Midget Gems out and offered me one.

I was a bit suspicious.

"Where have you been keeping these? It's not your special pantie hoard, is it?"

She said, "I just bought them new. You can open the packet and have any colour you like, even if it's not the top one."

Blimey, she is really pulling out all the stops.

On the way to Stalag 14
It's more fun being chummly wummlies with Jazzy Spazzy

than riding alone in the huffmobile.

I said, "Did you hear Wet Lindsay doing that ickle girl thing?"

Jas nodded like Noddy the well-known nodding dog from Nodland. And then she said, "I've decided I'm not going to go for being a prefect any more. I don't want to hang out with Wet Lindsay and ADM."

I said, "Who does? They don't even want to hang out with themselves."

But I was really pleased. I gave her a spontaneous outdoor hug. Even though we might have been seen by the Blunder Boys and created an outburst of "Get 'em off, you lezzies."

### Five minutes later

We were in such a good matey mood that we did the top part of the snot dance along the High Street... I am soooo happy I've got my luuuverly bestie mate and gang and on Saturday I will be in the arms of a Luuurve God. Probably.

### Break

We were in a spontaneous dance mood all day. But not in a getting-a-detention way. When Mr Attwood appeared around our camp (the fives court) in his wheelchair, we did a quick rendition of the snot dance. Just to cheer him up. In case he was feeling peaky at having to pretend to be crippled. But did he appreciate it? No, he did not.

In fact, as usual, he was shouting.

"You young buggers, I'll tell the headmistress about this!!"

I said, "Mr Attwood, we are merely trying to cheer you up with our girlish high spirits. Anyway, I am here to help. I am going to push you to the science block..."

He said, "I'm not going to the science block."

I said, "Are you sure?"

He didn't seem keen, but I started pushing his chair down the incline towards the lower part of the science block.

I said, "Oooh, we're really moving along now, aren't we, Mr Attwood? Are you enjoying yourself? I am."

He was yelling, "Oy oy, watch it, watch it!!!"

Then we started going faster and faster and I was singing, "He taught me to yodel... yodo-le-ee-heee. Do you know *Heidi*, Mr Attwood?"

He was shouting, "Never mind about bloody *Heidi*!"

I said, "Never mind about *Heidi*? It's a classic, Mr Attwood... Oh dear, oh dear... Oh NO! I've lost control of the chair. I can't stop it... We're going to crash into the science block! Save yourself, save yourself!!!"

At which point, Mr Attwood leaped out of his chair like a very old startled earwig. He was trotting along, pulling up his trousers and grumbling on, "Bloody fool, I could have been killed!"

But I fell to my knees and started yelling, "It's a miracle. It's a miracle. Look, everyone. He can walk. He walks!!!!"

And loads of people saw him, so everyone knew he was pretending, so he didn't dare do anything to me. Resultio! He was bang to rights, as our proud bobbies in blue might say (if they were in the mood).

Afternoon break
I explained my re-entrancing a Luuurve God plan.

Rosie said, "So your nub and gist is nicey-nice, glaciosity and pouch work?"

"*Mais oui.*"

Friday evening
8:00 p.m.
In bed with a face mask on. I've made it myself with mashed

up banana and cream. It feels disgustingly slimy. Like having Wet Lindsay on your face. OH MY GOD!!!

I want to scrub my brain out.

I hope the Luuurve God appreciates this. Although, of course, I don't necessarily want him to know about me being slathered in banana.

**8:10 p.m.**

I am going to lie here in my mask and imagine what I want to happen tomorrow night. I've barricaded my door with some drawers, so it should be cat and loon proof.

Not that anybody cares what I'm up to, as it's party headquarters downstairs. Mum has got some of her mad aquarobics friends round and Dad and Uncle Eddie and their new bestie Mr Across the Road are all making complete arses of themselves.

They are all wearing tight, light blue jeans for a start. What is that all about? Where have all the proper dads gone? Like in Dickens and so on. Dads in "Crap Expectations" and "David Copperpants" were either dead or had a proper job that kept them out of the house all day and most of the night.

My only idea of what a real dad could be like comes from Jas's dad. He wears Marks and Spencers casual slacks and a cardigan with a pocket for his pipe and bifocals. Like in the *Good Dad Guide Book*, which I haven't read and Dad certainly hasn't. And if I had read it, I know for a fact there would not be a chapter on "How to be a male stripper".

Anyway, where was I?

Aaaah, yes, relaxey vousey and Ohhhhmmmmmm...

Here we go and relaxxxxxxxxxxxxxxxxxxx...

So, here I am in my fantasy. I have arrived at the Sugar Club. Hmmmmm, I looked naaaice in my mum's fabby stilettos and my denim skirt and little cheeky waistcoat which emphasises my shape, but doesn't thrust my basoomas into the face of others.

My hair displayed *magnifique* bounceability and my skin glowed with the look that only four bananas mashed to a pulp can achieve.

Confident of my charms, I blinked my eyes slowly (forty-five layers of mascara are heavy). My nose, which once flung itself with gay abandon across my face, seemed a normal size. I have quite literally grown into my nose. Although this is not to suggest that I have an enormous head.

And when I say I have grown into my nose, I also don't mean that I am actually living in my nose, so stop it. And get out of my fantasy, whoever you are.

My Ace Gang and I entered the club and everyone looked round. Who is that, they asked themselves. She looks like someone who should go out with a lead singer or something... The band came on and started to play.

I was dancing by myself. I don't need a partner tonight because... there he was.

Up on the stage.

In the spotlight of life.

A Luuurve God.

And everyone knows that a Luuurve God on the stage is worth two on a bus.

He looked at me. I looked at him.

Time stood still.

Suddenly, he got his maracas out (leave it) and started playing. It was a tune called "Georgia, *mia bellissima*, Georgia".

It was about me.

He beckoned me on to the stage.

I looked shyly away, but the crowd started chanting, "We want Georgia, we want Georgia!!"

Smiling sweetly, I got up on to the stage. But I couldn't sing – why was I up there?

The Stiff Dylans started to really rock out. Robbie gave me a nice smile and nodded his head to me.

Suddenly, I knew what I was born to do.

I started to move to the beat.

I raised my arms and *WHOOOOSH*!

Flame dance to the right, flame dance to the left.

*Whoosh whoosh.*

The Ace Gang looked at each other and, smiling shyly, they too mounted the stage (I said leave it).

They acknowledged the crowd with a quick huddly duddly and then they joined in with the dancing...

We did a compilation of our greatest hits, flame to the right, flame to the left.

*Whoosh whoosh.*

Bogey dangle, bogey dangle.

Eyes shut for night-time Viking paddling,

Paddle, paddle to the right and to the left,

Then interweaving paddling.

And then, in a grand finale, we fell to our knees with a shout of HOOOORRRRN!!!!

As the crowd went wild, Wet Lindsay got her coat. A beam of light from the stage illuminated her lack of forehead. She beckoned to Robbie and he shook his head. She stormed off.

The Luuurve God helped me to my feet and stared in admiration. I knew what he was thinking (telepathically). "Aaaaah, beauty-io and talent-io all in one package-io."

He kissed my hand and then all up my arm. And then he started on my neck.

Thank goodness he didn't start at my ankles otherwise we would have been there all night.

As he got to my ears, I saw Dave the Laugh in quite a cool suit. He was just looking at me sadly, then he said to Emma, "Get your face on, love, we're leaving."

He looked angry and upset.

Hang on a minute, how did Dave the Laugh get in this? And also why is he such a downer??

I sat up in bed. He's spoiled my fantasy now, stropping around in the Humpty Dumpty.

For no reason at all. Ish.

Boo.

## Two minutes later

I should have told him about the Titches' tribute to him when they broke the loo seat. That would have cheered him up. It's not like him to be moody. He's not an Italian Stallion.

In fact, that's one of the best things about him, that he is Dave the Laugh.

The key word being "Laugh".

## One minute later

I wonder who Jas likes best out of Dave the Laugh and Masimo?

She's never said.

I might phone her and ask her.

Not that I am bothered.

## In the hall
## 9:00 p.m.

I can hear the "grown-ups" giggling like fools. I glanced into the front room to see Dad crawling through Mum's friend, Big Beryl's, legs. He had a balloon in his mouth. It is very disturbing.

I went to use the phone and Mum came mumming out.

I said to her, "Mum, this is not some sort of wife-swapping party, is it? Because if it is, can I not have Big Beryl as my new mum?"

Mum said, "Don't call her Big Beryl."

I said, "You do."

And she said, "Yeah, but not in front of her."

That is sooo typical of the lax morals she has.

### Thirty seconds later

Rang Jas.

Jas's mum, who is practically a saint in human form in my opinion, answered the phone. She even sounded glad to hear my voice – that is how nice she is. When I asked for Jas, she said, "I'll get her. She is just making an aquarium with Tom."

For politenessnosity I said, "Are you doing anything nice this evening?"

And she said, "Well, yes, Dad and I are jam-making actually."

I said, "I hope you've got your aprons on."

And she said, "Oh yes, dear."

And I know she does not lie.

As Mum passed again, staggering under the weight of

wine and lager, I said, "Jas's mum and dad are making jam."

She said, "Why is your face all slimy?"

Jas came on the phone all breathless and excited.

"Hi, hi, we've just put the gravel in and the miniature Ferris wheel. There's going to be a grotto area and..."

"Jas, fish don't go on Ferris wheels."

"Oh, I know that. It's for the crabs."

I didn't know what to say.

She went rambling on because she has little real idea of how mad she is.

"Anyway, what do you want? Have you decided what to wear? I've started learning my Juliet part. It's terribly sad."

You're not kidding, matey.

For friendlies sake, I pretended to be interested.

"Have you got to 'hark what pants through yonder windows break'? I like that bit – it's my fave."

She was, as usual, being Mrs Fussy Knickers.

"It's Romeo who says that and it isn't 'pants' it's 'light'..."

"Light, pants, owls... what difference does it make? I can't stand here discussing pants with you all night. I want to ask you a vair important question."

"What?"

"Who would you go out with? The Luuurve God or Dave the Laugh?"

"Oh nooooooooooooo, no, no, no and no. I am not answering that. You'll blame me for choosing the wrong one whichever one I pick, and anyway, it's nothing to do with me."

"Come on, Jazzy, I just want to know. I won't blame you or anything. I love you."

"Don't start that again."

"Come on, Jas."

"You promise you don't mind and you just want me to be honest? From my point of view?"

"Yep, as simple as that."

"Hmmmm."

There was a silence.

Apart from what sounded like chewing.

What was she chewing?

I bet it was her fringe.

I said, "Hello, what are you doing? Look, just be spontaneous!!! It's a simple, harmless question. Who would you choose? There's no pressure, JUST CHOOSE!!!!

She said, "Well... Dave the Laugh of course."

"What? What did you say?"

"Dave the Laugh."

"But I'm going out with the Luuurve God. You know, the grooviest, most good-looking Pizza-a-gogo dreamboat."

"I know, but I personally and hypothetically would choose Dave the Laugh."

"Why?"

"He's a laugh."

"Masimo's a laugh."

"When?"

"Jas, me and him have LOADS of laughs when we are alone. We are practically laughing the whole time."

"Well, that's good. I'm just saying that I have seen you have a laugh with Dave the Laugh, but I haven't seen you have a laugh with Masimo. He's not called Masimo the Laugh, is he?"

I said, "Well, I have to go now, Jas. Goodbye."

"You've not got the hump, have you?"

"Of course I have not got the hump, I assure you."

Why did she say Dave the Laugh?

10:30 p.m.

I can't get to sleep now.

I know why Jas chose Dave the Laugh. It's because she's frightened of doing anything unconventional. She probably thinks that Masimo is not really English.

He isn't.

**11:00 p.m.**
If she had parents like mine, she'd probably choose someone a bit different.

**11:10 p.m.**
Anyway, Dave is the "different" one. You wouldn't get Masimo doing run run leap.

**11:15 p.m.**
Or swearing in German.

**11:16 p.m.**
Or doing mad twisting.

**11:24 p.m.**
Or nip libbling.

Right, that's it. I am going to sleep. I am giving my brain

an official warning.

I know what, I will distract myself by reading through my part in *Rom and Jule*. I suppose I will have to learn it sometime.

I may as well get into the mood to be Mercutio.

I will climb into the tights of life.

Right, here we go...

## Ten minutes later

Crikey. Miss Wilson said that Mercutio was the comedy part. He is supposed to be a laugh, but frankly, he's what I would call an "unlaugh". I may have to improvise some comedy moments with fake blood...

When I say "Ay ay a scratch, marry; tis enough. Where is my page? Go villain, fetch a surgeon," after I am stabbed to death, I could make fake blood spurt all over the page and they would be bound to have the ditherspaz and possibly fall off the stage.

Yes, I am beginning to see the possibilities of Billy Shakespeare's renowned comedy... Zzzzzzzzzzzzzzzzzzzzzzz zzzzzzzzzzzzzzzzzzzzz.

# My tights runneth over

## Saturday September 24th

I feel much better and excited about seeing the Luuurve God again and impressing him with my sophisticosity.

I feel cool as a cucumber that has been lying around in a fridge, reading books on coolness.

### Phone rang

It was Jas.

"Where shall we meet? Hey, guess what? There's going to be an international band management type person coming tonight. If the Stiffs go on world tour, would you give up your education to go with them?"

"No, of course not. What is pleasure and travel and luuurve, compared to knowing how to say 'I have broken my glasses' in French?"

## In my bedroom

The only blot on the landscape of luuurvenosity is sneaking Mum's shoes out of her wardrobe without being thrashed to within an inch of my life.

I must not arouse her temperosity in any way. Especially since she has been in such a bad mood since the balloon party thing. I don't know what Dad has done, but she doesn't like it. I don't like it and I don't even know what it is.

Anyway, I must be like the wily fox.

Foxy and wily.

Here I go as a foxy-wily thing.

## In the kitchen

I said, "Do you want a cup of tea, Mum?"

Foxy wily, foxy wily.

She looked at me.

"Have you got my perfume on?"

I resisted the temptation to strop off and said, "No, it's just that well... I'm really excited about tonight, you know, making it up with Masimo and..."

She smiled at me.

"It's lovely being so into someone, isn't it? I remember when your dad used to..."

Oh no, she is going to talk about her feelings for Dad. I must stop her, and also get her to go out so I can get her shoes.

### Two minutes later

In a fit of hysterical madness, I have found myself agreeing to go to the Wild Park with her tomorrow.

How did that happen?

I just said, "You need to go out more." Now I'm going out with her.

I meant to get her shoes.

### In my bedroom

I have given myself a French manicure because that is vair vair European. And also because I don't know what an Italian manicure is.

Phone rang

Dad yelled up, "Georgia, it's another of your mates again. I am trying to work out a new dance routine with the magnificent baldy-o-gram and am constantly interrupted."

I didn't bother to reply.

He is wearing shorts around the house.

What if a normal person unexpectedly pops round?

He has leg hair that stops at his knees.

How grotesque.

I am beginning to feel a bit sorry for Mum.

It was Rosie.

"Sven has just cooked me a Viking snack."

"What is it?"

"Deep-fried Mars bar. I could paddle for miles now and still do a spot of pillaging and extreme violence at the end of it."

Just to check that my lecture on sophisticosity had got through to the Ace Gang I said, "What are you wearing tonight? There is no beard involved, is there?"

Rosie laughed, but not in a reassuring way.

"Toodle pip, see you at 7:30 p.m."

**6:00 p.m.**

Mum and Dad and Bibbs and Uncle Eddie have popped out to get a pizza in the loonmobile. I've just heard the roar of its massive quarter-horsepower engine *phut phut* off into the distance.

Before they went, I could hear Mum having a go at Dad in the driveway just under my window. She is deffo at No. 8, the quarter humpty (evils), on the Having the Hump Scale. Bordering on No. 9, the half humpty (evils and withdrawal of all snacks). This started because he didn't open the car door for her. She said, "Jim across the road has lovely manners – he opens doors for me."

Dad said, "Come on, love, you're a big woman, a very big woman. You can manage a little door. You could open it easily with one of your nungas."

I didn't hear the rest of it, but it was mostly Mum shouting and Libby yelling, "Bum bum, arsey ARSEEEEEEEY!"

Lovely.

**7:15 p.m.**

Got Mum's shoes, although they are not what you would

call comfortable. They are what you would call agonising.

I'll wear my ballet pumps till I get there.

Oh, I am so nervy. I nearly stuck the mascara brush up my nose. Oh God, I may be turning into Ellen. She's only phoned me eight times to tell me that she is soooo excited about seeing Declan. I think that is what she said. Or something. What do you think? Or something? Shut up!!!!!!

## Met the Ace Gang at Hennes

My worst fears are realised. Rosie is wearing a lurex catsuit...

She saw me looking and said, "Yes, it's groovy, isn't it?"

As we walked along, I said, "Please tell me that Sven has not got a matching catsuit."

She just winked at me.

Oh no, I bet he has.

And I bet it is snug.

Round the trouser snake area.

Oh noooooooo.

As we walked, I gave the gang the pep talk.

"Don't forget the plan. The key note here, is nicenosity

and glaciosity. You have to be around me at all times, making me look vair popular... Smiling is good, but no ad-hoc, full-on snorting and capering sort of laughing."

## Sugar Club
### 9:00 p.m.
We're going in.

It's an amazing place. It's got a sort of "chill out" room. I know that because it says so on a notice. Ellen was going, "Is it like... if when... you know, you're hot or something and..."

Ellen should really live in that room. She is so dithery at seeing her "boyfriend" that she can hardly keep her head on.

## In the tarts' wardrobe
I said, "I've got this new stay-on lipstick so even if someone had a wire brush, they couldn't get it off."

Rosie said, "Oh yeah, you say that but you should get Sven to test it. If anyone is a human wire brush, it's him. The gorgeous big brute."

I said, "Where is the gorgeous big brute?"

Rosie said, "With the lads. They are having a pre-club game of footie in the park."

It's dark.

Why?

## Ten minutes later

OK, big breaths (yeth, I thertainly have got big breaths. Shut up brain).

I've got my stilettos on. I am full to the tippy topmost of sophisticosity and *je ne sais quoi*.

Except in the knicker department, which has a touch of the jelloid about it.

What if Masimo has had second thoughts and he just comes over and says, "Face it, love, you're dumped"?

Although he of course would say "dump-io-ed".

## 10:00 p.m.

The Blunder Boys came lurgying in. Mark Big Gob had his hands in the back pockets of his jeans and some tiny fool hanging off his arm. His mouth is practically bigger than she is. As he passed by us, he said, "There's a party in my trousers and you're all invited."

And the Blunderers were going, "Oh yeah. Cool."

And laughing like constipated hyenas.

Prats.

10:30 p.m.

Oooh, this is agony, this hanging around pretending not to be hanging around. Where is he?

Then I saw him. He came out of the backstage area and he was wearing an electric blue suit with a blue shirt. Blimey, he looked so cool. And he's so sort of blokey. He's got a bit of designer stubble and his hair is a bit longer.

Every bit of me is separately jelloid. Now I know how Slim feels when all her chins are moving in a different rhythm.

He was talking to a group of St Pat's boys and then two tarts I vaguely knew from St Mary's came up, thrusting themselves at him. And giggling, like hens that had eaten too many worms and were having a worm rush. If you know what I mean and I think you do.

Mabs said, "You'd better move about a bit, Gee, otherwise he won't know you're here."

Jools said, "Look, there's a spare table. Let's go and sit down at it and then he will see us walking across."

Good point well made.

We started to walk over to the table.

Bloody hell, Mum's shoes were high. I'd better walk slowly. Oh, and do the flicky hair, hip to the right, hip to the left thing that boys are supposed to like. I don't know why they like girls who look like they have got false hips, but there you are. The whole bloody thing is a mystery.

### Two minutes later

It is amazing though, boys really do like it. At last I reached the table and put my hand on it to steady myself. I'm exhausted. I may have to have a little lie-down under the table and...

"*Ciao*, Georgia."

I looked up and there he was. Looking at me with those dreamy eyes. They looked amazingly yellow. It must be the blue suit, but they were sort of like Angus's eyes. Not insane, clearly, but the colour was the same. And his skin is sort of olive, and his mouth, well, blimey is all I can say.

### Thirty seconds later

So much for our plan of light sophisticated talk... the Ace

Gang were WUBBISH. They were just giggling and twittering on.

"Oooohhh, look at your nice shirt..."

"Ooooh, hahahha."

"Oooohh, I like your hair long it's... Ooooohhh."

Etc. like a bunch of mad doves.

Masimo said to me, "Miss Georgia, maybe at the end of the gig, I could walk you home."

Oh, thank God. He still liked me, at least a little bit.

I smiled at him (a contained smile, making sure that my nose didn't spread all over my face). I just smiled enigmatically and kept tight control over my nostrils. I wanted to say something, but I had lost all control of my bits and pieces.

My brain felt quite literally like a bag of wet mice.

He came and stood close to me and touched my face. He said, "Tonight there is, how you say, the men for management... they are wanting to speak with me in the break. So, *mi dispiace*, I will not be having you for myself until later... Sorry, *cara*..."

Then he kissed me softly on the hand and then behind the ear, and then two little kisses on my neck and then he looked me in the eyes – I was melting, I was melting – and put his mouth on mine. When he stopped, I came back to earth and saw the Ace Gang just looking at us. Masimo didn't seem to notice them. He stroked my hair and said, "*Cara*," and squeezed my bottom slightly as he left.

The gang were just silent after he had gone.

Then Rosie said, "Phwaooooor."

Jools, Mabs and Hons went, "Whooooooooaaaaaaah."

Jas said, "Cor."

And Ellen said, "He... that was... your ear... and er... so on."

I had to sit down quickly as the bottom part of me had turned into a jellyfish.

Ten minutes later

Jas tried to pretend that she had only said "Cor" because she was finding her inner passion as Juliet. Oh yeah.

As Billy Shakespeare would have said, "Prithee, lackaday and also WHATEVERS!!!!!"

I couldn't help saying to her, "Don't forget, you chose Dave the Laugh not the Luuurve God that you have just said 'Cor' to."

Jas went sensationally red.

"I knew this would happen. You said you hadn't got the hump, but you had. And I knew you would get it. I do not have the big red bottom for either of them. Hunky is my one and only."

I said, "Calm down, Jas. It's only the hypothetical red botty that you have got."

"I have not got the hypothetical red bottom. I haven't got the red bottom at all."

She has though.

As the band were tuning up and messing about with their equipment... oo-er (leave it), I tried to keep the conversation light and frothy so that I could tinkle with laughter and Masimo could see me out of the corner of his eye.

I said to Jas, "Speaking of *Rom and Jule*, has Miss Wilson found a Rom yet? Why can't we just have a bloke?"

Jas was glad to get back into boring rambling on about being a thespian. She said, "Miss Wilson says that in Shakespearian times there would be no women in the plays and so Juliet would have been played by a boy. And in our production, all the parts will be played by girls. She thinks it's an interesting reversal."

"Yes. But she is wrong. Anything she says is interesting is not. Think of the 'making our own musical instruments' fiasco. I had runner beans down my nick-nacks for weeks."

Rosie said, "Nauseating P. Green would make a cracking Romeo. She's got the glasses for it."

Jas went very red (tee-hee) and said, "Nauseating P. Green is one of the townspeople."

I said, "She could be all of the townspeople for all I care. The question is, who is going to be your boyfriend?"

Jas went even redder. She can never lie.

I said, "You KNOW, don't you, Jazzy? You know who your boyfriend is going to be!!!! Come on, tell."

She was getting redder and redder.

At that moment, Wet Lindsay and her silly "mates" came in. She went scampering over to the side of the stage and called Robbie to her. I don't think he really wanted to go. He is, of course, only human. I feel really sorry for him.

Astonishingly Dim Monica is not well-known for her fashion sense (the puffball skirt) but tonight she had outdone herself. Culottes are a bit of a risk anyway, but especially if your legs are only half a metre long. And your botty is a bit loomy. In fact, ADM looked like my vati in his shorts.

Jas was looking at them and manically fiddling with her fringe and suddenly it dawned on me.

I said, "It's not Astonishingly Dim Monica, is it? Oh, top!! Thank you, Baby Jesus!!!!!"

Jas was really red. She said, "No, don't be stupid. Of course it's not her!"

Then her eyes sort of swivelled to the stage.

Ohmygiddygodspyjamas.

No.

We all said, "No!"

But yes. Wet Lindsay.

Jas said, "It was Miss Wilson's idea."

I said, "Well, that's as maybe, but you must tell her that you cannot do it. It is against the European Code of Human Rights."

Jas said, "I did! I tried! I said, I said, I didn't want to be Juliet in that case, but then she was going to tell Slim and..."

As she was dithering and rambling on, Wet Lindsay came over to our table and said, "Hi Jas, great news about the play. I can only manage a few of the general rehearsals, but we ought to get together at mine for extras."

Then, only pausing to give me the look of death, she Octopussed off.

Jas was as red as I have ever seen her. And that is saying something.

Rosie said, "She wants you to go round to hers for 'extras', if you know what I mean. And I think we all know what she means."

Actually, it was quite funny in a way.

I said, "Oy, Jas, in the big snogging scene between Rom and Jule... what number do you think you will get up to with Wet Lindsay? Open mouth kissing with tongues?"

Jas was getting the defensive hump.

"Look, stop being so stupid. It's called acting – it's not snogging. It's only pretend snogging."

I said, "That's what you will say to Lindsay, but she won't take no for an answer. If she wants to do *Abscheidskuss* with you, she will."

Rosie leaped to her feet. "She might want to do *AUF GANZE GEHEN*!!"

And she started doing the flame dance around Jas. It was making me laugh a lot and not in a girlish, tinkling way. I was trying to pull myself together when Sven and the rest of the lads came in from their blind football.

### Ten minutes later
The Stiffs are playing a new one: "Tell me about yourself sometime". Robbie and Masimo are doing lead vocals. Wow, they both look cool. And one of them is my ex and one of them is mine mine miney mine mine. I am indeed the SEX KITTY of all England!!!!!

### Two minutes later
I'll tell you for free who does not think I am a Sex Kitty. Dave the Laugh. I saw him at the bar laughing with some of his mates and he caught me looking at him. And he stopped laughing and just nodded his head. Like I was just someone he knew, but didn't like that much. Then he turned his back on me and started talking and laughing again.

### Fifteen minutes later
I am sitting by myself because it's a slow number and the gang are all smooching with their boyfriends. Dave is dancing with Emma. He does smoochy smooch for a bit and

then every now and again does fast twisting to the floor and sort of Cossack dancing. He used to do that with me. Emma is really laughing, but she is not joining in. I would have joined in. Like in the old days.

I think I might go to the tarts' wardrobe until the song's over.

Five minutes later

When I came back in, the band were playing the last number of the set. It's called "Hold me back" and it's really wild. One of the St Pat's boys I see quite a bit of at the footie and at gigs and so on, came over. I think he's called Chunky, but I can't be sure. He is a bit chunky, but in a nice way. Anyway, he asked me to dance. I was going to say no, but then I thought, I'm not the Virgin of Rheims. It's only Dave I have to be cool about, so I said yes.

Three minutes later

Oh no. Sven has started doing the conga.

I'm deffo not going to join in...

Oh, I've joined in.

I am doing the conga.

My shoes are killing me and also I am about two metres high. Please don't let me fall over and display my nick-nacks to a Luuurve God and also a Sex God.

Also, Masimo is bound to notice that Sven and Rosie are wearing matching lurex catsuits. And that they are my mates.

I must escape to recapture my sophisticosity. I do not want to do a second round of conga where I end up in front of the stage next to Rosie and Sven in matching lurex catsuits.

At a convenient moment, as we passed the door to the loos, I slipped off. I said a quick "*adios*" to Chunky and flung myself into the tarts' wardrobe...

I stumbled in and took off my shoes. Ow ouchy ow ouch. Why can't Mum buy sensible shoes? She'll ruin my feet at this rate. I took my tights off and stuck one of my poor feet into the sink.

That's when I saw four eyes looking at me...

"What in the name of arse?"

It was the Little Titches.

From their hidey-hole beneath the sink they said, "Hello, Miss."

I said, "Will you stop calling me Miss. And what are you doing under the sink?"

They got up. Well, I think they did. They are so titchy, it's hard to tell.

The Ginger Titch said, "We shouldn't really be under this sink."

I said, "You can say that again."

And the other one said a bit more loudly, "We shouldn't really be under this sink."

Dear *Gott in Himmel*.

I said, "Well, why are you then?"

"We snuck in the back way because we wanted to see the band. We're not allowed to do anything at home. It's like prison. Our parents just watch what they want on television and we have to eat what they have and so on."

Yeah, it's tough out there.

Ginger went on, "Do you think we could sneak into the club behind you and just go and say hello to Dave the Laugh?"

The other one said, "We've got something we want to give him."

Aaaahhh. That is so sweet.

I said, "Have you made him a card or something?"

Ginger said, "No, we just want to do No. a quarter on the Snogging Scale with him."

What what????

I said, "What in the name of arse is No. a quarter on the Snogging Scale, and by the way, how do you know about the Snogging Scale?"

The littlest one went a bit red.

"Because we heard you in the loos. We were hiding in there one break and we heard you and made our own one up."

You see. And Slim says I do nothing to set an example to the youth of today!

I said, "Go on then, what is it?"

They both said together, "It's kissing hands."

Oooooooh. This I have to see.


Three minutes later

Came out of the tarts' wardrobe. Ouch, bloody ouchy ouch. I'm sure my feet have swollen up. I am without doubt the patron saint of Titches.

I saw Masimo and the Dylans talking to some big blokes in suits. They started going up the stairs to the mezzanine floor of the club. I suppose for a bit of privacy for their meeting. Masimo saw me and blew me a kiss. Robbie was behind him and he smiled at me too. Double resultio!! But then Wet Lindsay arrived on the scene and slimed up the stairs behind Robbie and put her hands over his eyes like a blindfold.

She said, "Guess who, babe?"

Ooohhhh, it was so full of embarrassmentosity. Robbie looked really uncomfortable because she was just hanging around his neck and the others were waiting to get on with the meeting. If she starts doing all that "Wickle Lindsay can't climb up the BIG stairs", we'll all have a communal throw-up.

In the end, he disentangled himself and Wet Lindsay went to the far end of the club.

Erlack.

How can Robbie stand it?


Two minutes later

Jas was sitting on Tom's knee, and as I came up to her, I heard her say, "I think the crabs are moving their little wheel."

I said, "Jas, go and distract your new boyfriend, Wet Lindsay, while I sneak the two Titches in to see Dave the Laugh."

♡

She said, "Why would I do that?"

I said, "Because you are an all-round tip-top egg. Isn't she, Tom?"

Tom kissed her cheek and said, "Yes, she is. But I'm very jealous of her new boyfriend."

Jas went all girlie and red. "Stop it, you two, it's just a play!"

I raised my eyebrows.

Jas quickly said, "Why do the Titches want to see Dave?"

"They want to do No. a quarter on the Snogging Scale with him."

Jas said, "There isn't a quarter."

I said, "There will be in a minute if you get your skates on. Please, Jazzy Spazzy, let the Little Titches get to No. a quarter with Dave. They are unhappy at home – they are not even allowed Jammy Dodgers."

In the end, Jas sloped off to do distracting-the-octopus work.

It'll cost me twenty-two million years of talking to her about Hunky going off to Hamburger-a-gogo land, but as I have said, I should really be knighted for my services to small humankind.

Four minutes later

The Titches are marching smartly behind me, being inconspicuous. If you think that hunching your shoulders and looking furtively around like mad hamsters is inconspicuous.

Dave was still at the bar, joshing with his mates.

No sign of Emma. She was probably off somewhere practising her smiling.

I was quite nervy now that we were actually behind him. I hadn't really thought about how it might go. What if he was genuinely horrible to me, in front of everyone?

Girdey loins, girdey loins.

The Little Titches were practically vibrating with excitement.

I tapped Dave on the shoulder.

"Dave, could I just have a word?"

He turned round and looked at me.

Now I deffo had the droop. He wasn't smiling – or talking. He didn't even have the good manners to say hello.

I said, "Well, erm, I've got the Titches with me."

They bobbed out from behind me and Dave smiled at them.

"Hello, little Sex Kittys."

They bobbed back behind me, but said together, "Hello, Dave the Laugh."

He was being nice to them, but not to me. I ploughed on. "They wanted to ask if they can do something for you."

Dave raised his eyebrows and then he looked at me and went, "Gnot nis nit?"

I said, "I beg your pardon?"

He looked at me again and went, "GNOT nis nit?"

It was like really crap ventriloquism, you know, when someone tries to say "bottle of beer" as a ventriloquist, without moving their lips, and it comes out "gottle og geer"?

Well, like that.

I said, "Dave, why are you keeping your mouth shut?"

Dave looked at me with his eyes very wide.

"Necoz nime nog sunosed nu sneek nu uuu."

What is he doing?

The Titches said, "He says he is not supposed to speak to you."

Oh, I see.

I said, "I never said don't speak to me."

"Nu nid."

"Dave, if you keep this up, we'll be here all night."

"Nay norry."

"Nay norry?"

Ginger said, "He says you have to say sorry."

Oh, *sacré bleu*. Oh, all right then.

I said, "I'm sorry."

Dave shook his head.

"Nay norry narti."

Nay norry narti? Were we doing some sort of crap Olde English songe? Were we going to start morris dancing and hitting each other with tambourines now?

Little Titch said, "He wants you to say sorry, Vati."

This was ridiculous.

Dave was just looking at me, sipping his drink. Leaning on the bar.

I said, "Oh, gadzooks, OK. I'm sorry – Vati."

Dave said, "Oh, hello, Georgia. I didn't see you hiding behind the Titches."

He is sooooo annoying. But anyway, at least he was talking to me again.

I smiled at him and he smiled back. He's got a lovely smile.

Shut up, brain.

Anyway, I had a mission.

"The Titches wanted to see you and do their tribute to you."

One of the Titches said, "We got a reprimand each for it."

Dave said, "Good girls."

In a lunatic way, it was quite touching to see the Titches do their little tribute.

They stood in front of him and did actions as they sang (badly):

"We love you, Dave the Laugh, we do" (nodding and touching hearts and pointing at Dave)

"When we're not near to you, we're blue" (pretend crying)

"We love you, Dave the Laugh, we do" (more nodding)

"Oh, Dave the Laugh, we love you!!!" (manic stamping and snogging of their hands).

They really snogged their hands, a bit like Libby with Mr Potato Head.

And also the stamping was truly manic. I'm not surprised they broke the toilet seat.

Dave is not often lost for words, but he acted as if he had never had small girls snogging their own hands in front of him before.

He was laughing and he said, "That was, and I am proud to say it... sensationally mad."

Then they went all red.

Ginger said, "Faaanks, Dave, you are the bestiest. Bye, Miss. Huddly duddly."

And off they scampered.

I felt rather proud.

I am like the Godmutti.

It was just me and Dave, as the rest of his mates had backed off when the Titches had started their tribute to him. They had sloped off to "impress" some girls that were being harassed by the Blunder Boys.

I said to Dave, "Fanks for that, Dave."

He said, "Forgive me if I'm right, but aren't we not talking to each other?"

"That's not what I said."

"It is."

"Well, I know, but I only meant until Masimo cooled down and got off the numpty seat."

"And has he? Or will he be attacking me with his hair gel when I go to the wazzarium?"

I didn't want to have to talk about the Luuurve God to

Dave. It made me feel funny, so I said, "I'm looking forward A LOT to *Rom and Jule*; comedywise I think it will outdo *MacUseless*. There might be clowns and for the *pièce* of resistance, Jas is going to snog Wet Lindsay."

That got his attention.

He said, "Now you're talking my language. I've always loved the Bird of Avon, as you know. I thought Melanie's basooma juggling was a triumph, but now, girl snogging? As Billy himself would have said, 'My tights runneth over'."

I started laughing.

Then Dave looked at me. Quite intensely. Whenever I get near him, I feel sort of hypnotised. Well, my lips do... They were puckering up without my permission... Nooooo. He looked down and away, and then he said, "It's not a topless production, is it?"

Just at that point Emma came back. All Emma-ish. Why is she so keen on everything? She gave me a hug and linked up with Dave. She said, "Hi, Gee. Is it all cool with Masimo? If I didn't have the best boy, I would say that he was deffo the fittest."

Then she turned and kissed Dave on the cheek. "But no one compares to the Hornmeister."

Dave smiled and I smiled. But I didn't really want to smile. And I don't think he felt on Cloud 9 actually.

I didn't want to hang around with the two of them. It felt a bit odd.

So I did S'laters.

And went into the tarts' wardrobe for a bit of a sit-down on the loo, feet up in the air sort of thing.

Is Dave happy with Emma?

She's so nice. ALL THE TIME.

Why is that?

Is she really nice, or is she just pretending to be nice so that everyone thinks she is nice?

As I was sitting there in the cubicle, Jas came in. I knew it was her because no one else could have such an irritating way of blowing her nose. On and on. Not just one little blow and have done with it. Sort of little ones and then a big trumpeting one.

I hobbled out of my cubicle and there she was, sitting on the sink. Looking all miz.

Oh no. Now we would have to talk about Hunky for the next millennium. Still, she had helped me with the Titches.

She said, "I can't do it. I can't snog her..."

I tried to cheer her up. I owed her really.

"But, Jas, look on the bright side. Think how great it will be when she commits suicide. It'll bring the house down. We could buy those football clacker things. Or come on doing some ad-hoc celebratory Scottish dancing."

Jas said, "You'll have been dead for fourteen scenes by then, it's OK for you."

I could see she was upset.

"Look, we just need to think of some sensible way of dealing with her. Perhaps a chemistry experiment that goes tragically wrong as she happens to be passing?"

Jas just looked at me.

Then I said, "I've got it, by George, I've got it!!! We extend the puppetry motif that Miss Wilson is so vair vair keen on and we suggest that Romeo and Juliet have massive papier mâché heads. So you never actually see your real head and the snogging is just a question of aiming your massive heads at each other."

Jas said, "I don't want a big papier mâché head."

I said, "I am only trying to help, Jas. If you don't want to be helped...

## End of the gig

Lurking around like Lurkio at the stage door. It's a bit nippy noodles. I am nervy, but sort of happy. Also, and I have to admit this, I am really, really happy that Dave is being OK with me. I hate it when he gets the monk on.

As I was just thinking that, he loomed up with Emma and a crowd of his mates.

One of the lads said, "Are you up for a late snooker needle match, Dave? Haven't seen much of you lately, mate."

Dave said, "Maybe actually."

Then Emma pulled on his hand. "Oy, Hornmeister, don't forget we've got an early start for the sculpture park tomorrow. Mum and Dad planned to set off at 9:00 a.m."

Sculpture park?

Mum and Dad?

I looked at Dave and raised my eyebrows. He looked back and as Emma pulled him away, he pretended to do crying.

He didn't seem a sculpture park sort of guy to me.

What did I know, though? I have just remembered I have accidentally agreed to go to the Wild Park tomorrow with my mum and look at horned budgies or whatever.

Rosie and the rest of the gang trolled off as soon as the Dylans came out. There was a bit of banter between the lads and it seems that the management stuff has gone well.

Masimo still hadn't appeared. I had Dave's voice in my head going "Emergency hair gel application". Shut up, Dave.

The Ace Gang were all linked up, singing, "Give me an H, give me an O, give me an R, give me an N, what are you giving me? The HOOOOOORRRRNNNN!"

Just then, I felt two arms around me.

"Aah, Miss Georgia, you are noodly nips as you say. Come here inside my coat."

And he opened his coat and snuggled me in. I could feel his heart beating. The other Dylans were leaving and shouting, "Nice one, talk on the blower tomorrow about the London gig."

What London gig?

Also where was I?

It was snugly in the coat and everything, but I couldn't tell what was going on. I popped my head up through the collar to breathe a bit, just in time to see Wet Lindsay tucking Robbie's scarf into his parka. Oh, leave him alone,

Slimy Head. I don't know if she thought-read, but she turned round and gave me the worst look.

Poor Robbie.

Poor Jas. Who would want a boyfriend like Wet Lindsay? I must help both of them.

We scootered home through the twinkly night. The streets were quite busy and in fact we passed the Ace Gang still all linked up. Seeing them trying to get past a bloke walking his dog was hilarious. As we passed by them, Masimo sounded his horn and they all yelled back, "Hooorn!"

Masimo laughed and pulled my arms around him tighter. Blimey, this was a bit like having a real relationship, like you read about. I hope I know how to do it. If my mutti and vati were anything to go by, Masimo would be wearing enormous pants by the end of the week. I couldn't imagine Masimo in enormous pants. I bet he's got those really groovy Pizza-a-gogo ones... Stop thinking about his pants!!!

When we got back to my place, it was a beautiful clear night and the moon was beaming down at us. Like a big smiling custard pie in the sky. If you have seen one of those.

Masimo stopped his scooter at the bottom of our road so

that there could be no spying or "joining in" from my parents. Also I took Mum's shoes off and put on my flats when I got on the scooter. (I suggested that I had brought my "scootering shoes" with me to Masimo. Which I think is rather sophisticated.)

**12:30 a.m.**
We're sort of snuggled behind a hedge. Or Snog Emporium, as I call it.

Blimey, snogging Masimo is like going to Heaven in a bread basket and back.

And I don't even know how I would get into a bread basket. But that is luuurve for you.

Masimo whispered a lot of Italian stuff to me. It sounds so romantica and groovio gravio.

Of course, he might have been saying, "I can see a bogey up your nose."

I must learn some more Pizza-a-gogo-ese because conversation is a bit tricky in between the snogging.

**Ten minutes later**
The snogging is deffo top drawer though.

I wonder how far he got on the Snogging Scale with his ex?

Shut up, brain, just snog.

### Five minutes later

I like it that he kisses so softly and gently uses his tongue. Not like Whelk Boy, when it was like being attacked by whelks.

### Two minutes later

We even touched tongues and sort of kissed with them. Blimey. It's fabaroonie to learn new stuff about the game of luuurve.

Also I do like his hand technique... He put one hand on the back of my neck and one on the base of my spine. It made all of my body feel sort of linked up to him. Yum.

### Two minutes later

Something horrific happened. We were doing No. 5 when I heard the unmistakable sound of a lunatic shouting in the dark.

I looked carefully round the hedge and up our street. It

♡ 155

was Mr Next Door, in his shortie nightgown. He was shouting and the Prat brothers were yapping.

There is something a bit funny about the Prat brothers (besides the obvious fact that they are poodles)... In the moonlight, they look sort of dark blue with white things stuck on them.

Masimo said, "*Come?* What is that?"

I whispered, "That is Mr Next Door going barmy."

Masimo pulled me back into the Snog Emporium. And he kissed me so hard that all the blood drained from my head and went into my ballet pumps. Through the love daze, I could vaguely hear things kicking off.

Mr Next Door was raving on.

"He's a bloody disgrace. They've got a show tomorrow, I've been dyeing them all day. Now they're covered in feathers."

What was he on about?

I had to have a look.

We crept up along the hedge a bit so we could see.

Mr Next Door had a broom and a shovel. And he was standing at our gate. I heard a door being opened and then more shouting.

"What the bloody hell is going on?"

Oh no. I recognised those mad tones. It was my vati.

Then another voice joined in.

"Don't worry, Bob, I'm right behind you... oo-er."

Oh dear God. Uncle Eddie.

I said to Masimo, "Erm, I'd leave now if I were you. This is going to get ugly."

And that's when my vati and Uncle Eddie hove into view. Both wearing undercrackers.

The Luuurve God whispered, "Is that, er, your father, and is that, how you say, his boyfriend?"

I nearly shouted out, "NOOOOOOO, that's not his boyfriend!"

Four minutes later

I eventually persuaded the Luuurve God to leave. It took a bit of kissing and pleading. I don't think he really understood what was going on. Who could?

I've said it once and I will say it again, why can't everyone just speak English? The Americans give it a bit of a go – why can't other nations?

In the end, after kissing all of my fingertips, he crept off.

157

By this time, lights were coming on in the street. I took a deep breath as soon as I heard Masimo scooter off and came out from the bushes.

As I passed Mr Next Door's gate, Angus and Gordy dropped on to my head from the wall. They didn't hurt themselves though, because they gripped on to my shoulders with their horrible sharp claws.

I couldn't help it. I yelled out, "Oh, buggering buggeration."

Dad heard me and yelled, "Stop that bloody foul language, young lady. You'll wake up the sodding neighbourhood."

Oh, the irony.

Uncle Eddie said, "Evening, Georgia," as if it was teatime.

I said, "Look, we all want to go to bed. Is there something we can do to clear this up? What have your poodles done to frighten Angus and Gordy? Cats are very sensitive, you know."

Mr Next Door practically had a fit. He couldn't speak.

Dad could, sadly.

"Don't you start, young lady. Get yourself in the house!"

I didn't mind going in actually. Angus and Gordy had

both fallen asleep on my shoulders and they are not anorexic. It was like having a huge snoring fur coat on.

The front door was open. And my mum was hiding behind it.

She said quietly, "What the hell is going on?"

I said, "It's unbelievable! Vati and Uncle Eddie are both in their undercrackers."

She came out from behind the door.

And she was wearing a shortie black negligee.

What is this? Desperate Husbands?

I looked at her and said, "To be frank, I feel let down by all of you. I'll just say goodnight, Mother."

As I went up the stairs, she said, "Hang on a minute – those are my bloody Chanel shoes in your bag!!!"

Damnity damn damn.

How much shouting can one family do???

And what a bloody fuss about nothing. Angus had, from the kindness of his own heart, taken a gift into the Prat Poodles' kennel. All right, it was a half-alive pigeon that was probably flapping about a bit. And yes, the Prat brothers had fallen into the pond as they tried to escape. But what normal person dyes their poodles blue?

And then complains if they fall into a pond that THEY built?

That is the question.

**1:30 a.m.**

It's all gone quiet now, thank the Lord.

What a fiasco of a sham. At one stage, there was shouting inside and outside my house.

Even Libby woke up and shouted through the open window and threw Mr Cheese at Mr Next Door before she snuggled back into bed... My bed.

I tried to get in as well, but Libby, Gordy, Angus and Mr Potato Head were all sleeping horizontally. In the end, I went into Libby's bed.

I had to feel my way in the dark.

I didn't turn the light on because I really didn't want to see her sheets. I'll just say this: they crackled when I got in. And my feet touched something soft at the bottom. Pray God it was playdough...

# How to Make Any Twit Fall in Love With You

## Sunday September 25th

**Morning**

Mutti and Vati are not speaking to each other...

It was all, "Would you ask your mother to pass me the butter?" etc.

So childish.

Still, I had a Luuurve God, so what did I care? I was just about to go up to my room for a bit of a daydream about our poptastic lives together when Dad said, "Will you explain to your mother why Uncle Eddie and I were in the garden in our underpants?"

I said, "Certainly, Father. Mum, Dad is going out with Uncle Eddie. Face it. Move on."

Dad hit me over the head with his newspaper.

"Tell her we were practising a new routine for the baldy-o-gram when the fool next door started..."

Mum interrupted. "Tell your father I am sick of his japes with his pals."

I said, "She says you should go and live in a house with men like yourself and leave us alone. We'll write."

That did it.

Dad has "roared" off in his "car".


In my room

Where every clud has a silver lining. Dad "roaring" off having the numpty means that we won't be able to go to the Wild Park to look at more horned budgies etc.

I'm distracting Libby from poking Bum-ty with a fork with cheese on it, by reading her *Heidi* in a Chinese accent. She is hysterical with laughter. It's making me laugh actually. I do love my sister. There is something so gorgey about her little dimply face. She's got amazingly long eyelashes.

When we got to the famous wheelchair falling off the mountain top bit she looked up from laughing and then said, "I lobe my funny Gingky." And gave me a really big cuddle.

Blimey, it brought tears to my eyes.

Especially as Libby accidentally stabbed me with her fork.

### Ten minutes later

I could hear Mum on the phone, and then she called up the stairs.

"Georgia, get dressed. We're off on our lovely trip to the Wild Park."

Oh God.

### Twenty minutes later

We are off to the Wild Park with two of Mutti's mates, Pippy and Scottish Jo. They picked us up in their car. Wow, I am actually riding in a proper car that people don't point to and laugh at. Also it's quite peaceful because Mum, Pippy and Jo just talk all the time. Libby is combing what is left of Panda. She tried to warm him up by putting him in the oven. Most of his bottom is burnt to a crisp. She is happy though.

Gor blimey, Mum and her mates talk WUBBISH. I am glad that me and my mates are not so superficial. They are just talking about men and clothes and men.

I can just dollydaydream about my boyfriend and what I will wear when I next see him.

I must say, I can't really believe that he likes me.

And really fancies me.

Wow.

I'm a bit tired from last night and my lips ache a bit.

In a nice way.

I wonder if you can strain lips by too much snogging?

Jas said she did once. She got a sort of pucker spazerama.

Didn't she do puckering exercises for it?

Pucker relax.

Pucker relax.

Two minutes later

Erlack, she will soon be kissing Wet Lindsay unless something good happens.

Maybe I could suggest to Miss Wilson that we do mime kissing?

I am a genius!! Miss Wilson loves mime.

I wonder if Rudi and Miss Wilson have snogged yet?

### Fifteen minutes later

Even though I am trying not to listen, Mum and her mates are going to join this women's group that teaches you how to become a goddess and make men do anything for you. Crikey.

It sounds a bit like *How to Make Any Twit Fall in Love With You.*

Apparently, the nub and the thrust is that men *like* to do stuff for women. So, you ask them to do something and then you say thank you. And that is how you train them.

I said, "Are there any dog biscuits involved?"

But they were too full of themselves to reply.

### Wild Park

Wow and wowzee wow. We had the tippytop of times. Honestly. When we got there, I said I was very happy to stay in the car.

I said, "I've seen a bison on *Look North* or something and also some monkeys that Lady Dave Attenborough was lolling about with and that will do me, thank you."

But I was glad as a glad thing on glad tablets that Mum made me get out.

Because we found Angus's wild family.

Honestly.

His Scottish wildcat cousins.

They were sooooo cool. The kittens looked just like Angus when I first found him in the garden in Och Aye land. Doing flying face-pouncing. One kitten would unexpectedly and for no reason hurl itself through the air and pounce directly on another kitten's face. Then it would grab on with its front paws and do bunny kicks with its back legs.

Libby kept yelling, "Me want naaaice pussycats" and trying to climb into their cage with them.

One of the keepers said, "They are not pets. They are wild animals."

I said, "You don't need to tell me that. I used to keep Angus on a lead, but he ate it. Let us in, mister."

Libby even said, "Please, Mr arsey man."

Ten minutes later
We're in!!!

Oh, what a hoot. Libby and I had a bucket each of dead chicks and some rabbit legs.

We tugged on one end of a rabbit leg and the kittykats pulled on the other end. In between spitting at us.

I love them I love them.

We took some pictures to take home with us to show Angus what his family look like and also a little tartan mousey.

Mum and her mates were ridiculously embarrassing around the keepers who were quite fit, in an overall and welligoggy way...

### On the way home
Libby is "feeding" tartan mousey with bits of chicken feather she has stuffed in her welligogs. I hope that is all she has down there. She was very interested in what the wild kittens' poo looked like.

### 5:30 p.m.
When we got home, Dad wasn't in so Mum went off to have a bath.

She is sensationally cheered up and all full of herself now.

I said, "What's for supper?"

And she said to me, "Find something in the fridge. And give some to Bibbs. She's allowed to watch children's TV for half an hour. I'm having a long aromatherapy bath. I will use ylang ylang, I think, for its sensual overtones."

I said, "Mum, you don't need sensual overtones, you need sensual undertones."

She didn't get it though, she just went rambling on.

"This is 'me' time."

And she went off into the bathroom.

Ten minutes later

I made Bibbs and me cheese on toast, but remembered that we must eat a balanced diet, so put some tomato sauce on for the vit. C content. If my legs start getting all bendy like Grandvati's because of rickets, I hope Mum will find her ylang-ylang-smelling skin a comfort.

Libby is sharing her cheese on toast with tartan mousey. They are watching "Pudsey and Sudsey go on holiday" or something. Anyway, weird creatures with no necks in bathing suits.

As I left, she went to get her swimming costume and rubber ring. She lobes Pudsey and Sudsey's holiday.

In my bedroom
Ten minutes later

Mum's not the only one who can have "me" time. I can have "me" time for me to have some "me" time.

Aaaah... soooo, the Luuurve God.

I'll start with the tongue-kissing episode and...

"GET OUT! Ooooooh, how disgusting. Don't stand on there, you'll..." *SPLASH!!!!!*

Then more yelling and splashing and Mum saying, "Don't let it touch my... Ohmygod, it's touched me... Put that snorkel, owwww..."

MIAOOOOWWWWWW...

"Lalalalalala...... Heggyheggyho..."

What the hell was going on?

Four minutes later

Mum's "me" time turned into "us" time.

I went down to see what had happened and there was water everywhere in the bathroom. Mum was standing in a bath towel, shouting. Libby was in her swimming costume with a snorkel, sitting in the bath singing "Bum bum pooey pooey bum bum" in two centimetres of water. And Angus and Gordy were sneezing and soaking and trying to scrabble up the sides of the bath.

Mum stormed off into her bedroom and I said to Libby, who was now putting her rubber ring on, "What happened, Bibbsy?"

She looked at me cross-eyed, like I was a fool, and said very deliberately, "Me came on my HOLIDAYS wif my fwends. Get in, Gingie."

### Back in my bedroom

All is calm again.

I will get into my bed to look at my part (oo-er) in *Rom and Jule.*

Lovely and snugly, I may just have a little zizz before I settle down to...

Not.

Have you any idea what it is like to have two wet cats, a soaking tartan mouse and a toddler covered in soap in your bed?

### Fifteen minutes later

Libby has dried off a bit now and the cats have bogged off to murder stuff. They only stayed in my bed long enough to get warm and dampen the sheets.

Libby still has her rubber ring on, but it could be worse, she could have Mr Fish in here with us.

### Three minutes later

It IS worse.

She has got Mr Fish in here with us.

### Five minutes later

If I hear "Maybe it's beCOD I'm a Londoner" one more time, I may have a nervy spaz.

### Three minutes later

Mr Fish's batteries went. I will never be mean about Baby Jesus again.

Also I was just saying to Libby that she should lie down and have a little snooze when she dropped off to sleep, sitting up.

Amazing.

I carried her to her own room, which wasn't very easy actually with the rubber ring, but it does mean I have the whole of my bed to myself!!!!

**Ten minutes later**
Now then, back to Billy Shakespeare land. Otherwise known as "Twits in Tights".

**Ten minutes later**
Mercutio just lurks around Rom, more or less telling him off and then dies. I am going to call him Merc-lurk-io.

**Twelve minutes later**
I wish I could be bothered to get up and phone Jas. In Act 11 she has a whole night of snogging with her boyfriend, Wet Lindsay. She will have got further on the Snogging Scale than she has with Hunky. I bet she wishes she hadn't been so mean about my brilliant papier mâché head idea now.

She is vair stubborn.

Right, I am going to get some shut-eye.

**10:32 p.m.**

Oh, how vair vair inconsiderate some people are. I can hear Mum's voice booming all over the house. She is on the blower to one of her mad aquarobic mates.

Mum said, "Well, I'm deffo going to do it. At the very least it will shake Bob up, and stop him being so bloody lazy. Madame Betty said be there at 7:00. The workshop actually starts at 7:30 p.m... What? Oh, yes, OK, look, I'll just get the list, hang on."

I heard the phone being put down and Mum going off somewhere.

Oh, really, some people are trying to sleep.

I could hear her scuffling around.

I shouted down, "Mum, it is a school night you know. Some of us are trying to sleep."

Libby shouted from her bedroom, "Shut up, Ginger."

**One minute later**

Mum was just going on and on.

"Right, you've to bring a towel, a sarong to wear... it says you can keep your pants on if you wish. Erm... some coloured scarves and a boiled egg. Yep, yep. Oh and some oil. OK, see you there... S'laters."

God. Her workshop thing sounds horrific. What do a boiled egg and coloured scarves have to do with being a goddess? It sounds more like one of Miss Wilson's improvised drama workshops. Although, thank the Lord, Miss Wilson has never said, "You can keep your pants on if you wish."

How utterly horrific.

### Ten minutes later

Oh, that reminds me, I mustn't forget to ask Miss Wilson about fake blood for my dying scene.

We've got another read-through on Thursday. I wonder if Jas's new boyfriend will be there. She might be. Maybe I could accidentally chop her head off with my sword.

### Two minutes later

Ouch. I just leant on my pouch by mistake. I must remember to replenish my supplies. You must never be caught with an empty pouch.

### Phone rang

Oh, this is so selfish!!!!

I yelled down, "Mum, will you please not discuss your lady parts on the phone with your friends. I have an artistic temperament."

Mum yelled up, "Georgia, it's Masimo, or are you asleep for school tomorrow?"

Ohmygod.

I tore out of bed and quickly applied a bit of lippy from my pouch. I did a bit of puckering up on the way down the stairs so that he could sense my Sex Kittykatnosity down the phone.

(Oo-er!)

Picked up the phone and...

"Hello."

"*Ciao, cara*, I just have phoned to say..."

Then he started singing a song down the phone. Something in Italian. Also he was playing the guitar as an accompaniment. How was he holding the phone? Perhaps he had an assistant?

It's nice and everything, but what do you do? Nod along to it? Join in? I was just holding the phone away from my earlug, because it was a bit loud, when the key turned in the lock and Vati came in. And he looked at me with the phone and a song coming out of the end of it.

He said, "Don't tell me there's a bloody singing clock now."

And stumbled off into the bedroom.

## Monday September 26th
### In the kitchen
I noticed an egg boiling away. I can't even begin to think what Mum and her mad mates are going to be doing with that.

### On the way to Stalag 14
How many times do we all have to do this? Get up, go to school, again? Before everyone admits it's a crap idea?

### Break
Thank the Lord.

### Fives court
Brrr! Blimey O'Reilly's trousers, it's nippy noodles.

We've buttoned our coats together like in the old days. We are quite literally a tent with six heads and sleeves.

## Three minutes later

Snuggly buggly. We have to sort of thread the snacks up to our mouths through the collar bits.

Rosie and Jools made me laugh a lot by doing duo Twix eating. One started at one end and the other at the other end. Vair amusant. And as Rosie said, "Strangely erotic."

Wet Lindsay came by, but apart from tutting at us, what is she going to punish us for? Coat abuse?

She said, "The rest of them I am not surprised at, but I am sorry you have chosen to join in, Jas."

Jas didn't say anything, but after Ms Slime had gone off we all went, "Oooooooohhhhh" like in "Oooooooohhh, get you!"

## Geoggers

We are doing about deserts.

What would you do to survive if you got stranded in one?

I said, "Phone a friend?"

But, as usual, I got *nuls points* for my hilarious sense of fun and adventure.

It's all so tremendously dull. You have to put your car mirrors out to catch the sun and blind any passing plane etc. Dig a ditch and lie in it. Dear God, just kill me, that's what I say.

Jas, of course, is in Seventh Heaven.

Her hand was shooting up all the time.

Saying stuff like, "You could catch water at night because of the diurnal change in temperature."

Oh, SHUT UP!!!!

Just as I thought I might have to pull my own head off to stop the boredom, Rosie passed me a questionnaire that she had made up.

Dear All,

Suppose you were stranded on a desert island with your family and with no food. Not even Jammy Dodgers. Who in your family would you eat first? Here are a few ideas.

Who does least work?

Who eats most?

Who would make the most nutritious meal?

Who would be the easiest to track down and catch?

And my answer to all of the questions was: Dad.

## PE

As a "treat" and because the weather is so bad, Miss Stamp has allowed us to stay indoors. It's a miracle really because she is such a sadist. Once she made us play hockey in the fog. You couldn't see your hand in front of you. You'd hit the ball off in the general direction of where you thought someone was and then go after it, if you heard someone go "Owwwww".

When I reached the goal, the goalie had wandered off into the fog somewhere. By the time she got back I had scored 19 goals, but Miss Stamp disallowed them.

Which is typical.

When I protested she said, "Georgia, no one else was playing, you were just running about by yourself and shooting goals into an empty net. That is not hockey."

I said, "Well it's my kind of hockey!!!"

She said I had taken stupidity to new heights, which is a bit rude.

Anyway, happy days. Today, as our special "treat", we are playing shipwreck in the gym. While everyone else dashed about, the Ace Gang all climbed to the top of the wall bars. You're supposed to leap about from a piece of equipment to a mat to a whatever, but unless Miss Stamp actually came up the bars and removed us, we were technically safe.

Anyway, she didn't notice at first because Nauseating P. Green created an accidental diversion by destroying the mini trampoline.

While we were hanging about, we had a discussion about the fact that we all now had boyfriends.

Jas said, "I feel like I've known Tom all my life. I feel we have always been together."

I said, "So do I."

Rosie said, "It's just a complete laugh with Sven."

I said, "Yes, but do you feel natural?"

Rosie said, "You'll have to ask Sven that, love!"

And laughed like a drain.

I said to the others, "But what I mean is, besides the

snogging... what do you actually do with boys when you've got them?"

Ellen said, "I well... how do you really know if you've got them or something... you know... what if you haven't got them or something..."

I said, "Thank you for that, Ellen. It's cleared it up for me."

## Changing rooms

Getting changed. My brain is still burbling on.

Should I see my "boyfriend" every day? Or every two days?

Is the Luuurve God going to sing to me every night?

Am I supposed to phone him and sing to him when it's my turn?

Could I do an improvised dance instead?

How do you know these things?

Why am I expected to do lessons as well as boy stuff?

## 4:00 p.m.

Bell went.

Thank the Lord. Freedom.

### Cloakroom

I was just getting my coat on when Jools came in. I thought she'd gone home. She was a bit breathless.

"Gee, I've just run all the way back. Masimo is at the gate on his scooter."

*Ay caramba!!*

Look at my head!

### Eight minutes later

Emergency make-up routine and upside-downy blowdrying hair. I have made the gang surround me so that I can get to the gate without my beret. It may look a bit odd, us all walking like a big crab, but that is the penalty of luuurve.

And it does mean that I can emerge with hair bounceability in front of my boyfriend (oo-er).

Masimo was sitting on the seat of his scooter with his legs crossed. He had jeans and Chelsea boots on and a long cardigan.

He said to the gang, "*Ciao.*"

And they all said "*Ciao*" back.

Then we stood around a bit.

Erm.

Masimo came and stood in front of me. He put his hands on my face and kissed me on the mouth. Then he said, "Hello, gorgeous."

And he snogged me properly. I had my eyes open because I felt a bit, erm, unrelaxed with 500 girls passing by.

The gang were shuffling about behind me, I could sense it and then Jas said loudly, "Well, I'm off... er, are you off, Rosie?"

And Rosie said, "Er, yes, I'm off, off as, erm, anything."

And they were all saying even more stupid things than normal.

"*Hasta la vista.*"

And "Toodle pip."

After they had all gone, Masimo was still just casually stroking my hair and kissing me softly on the lips.

I didn't want to push Masimo away, but... it was all a bit weird. I just wanted to get away from Stalag 14.

At last I said, "Erm, shall we go?"

And he smiled and gave me a last big smacking kiss.

Just then, I caught sight of an elephant in a coat out of the corner of my eye.

Oh dear God, Slim.

I looked away.

Masimo gave me another smackeroonie and then put a helmet on my head.

And we roared away.

Perhaps it had really been an elephant in a coat. Perhaps it was a special surprise for the production of *Rom and Jule*.

You never know.

Ish.

## Café Noir

Actually, it was quite cool being the "girlfriend" when Masimo's mates and so on came into the café.

It is mostly band talk though.

In fact, Masimo had to drop me off home and go talk to the band round at Robbie's about their London gig.

Which is this coming weekend.

Am I a pop widow already?

## 10:00 p.m.

Learning my part for the school fiasco. AGAIN. I thought Merc-lurk-io was supposed to be the "larf" factor. All I can say, once more, is that Billy Shakespeare had a very odd idea of fun.

Oh dear God.

This is wubbish jokes.

Mostly I describe the Queen of the Fairies for about a million years. Apparently, all she does is drive along in a tiny wagon "over men's noses as they lie asleep".

They wouldn't be asleep for long if someone drove a wagon over their nose. I tell you that for a fact.

Because, as it happens, I have had a wagon driven over my nose. When I was asleep. Libby put Gordy in her Thomas the Tank Engine when he was a kitten and made him drive up the "big big hill" (my nose).

### Twenty minutes later

Oh, this is just wubbishnosity of the highest order. I can't go on in tights and say this:

"Her waggoner, a small grey-coated gnat."

### Three minutes later

Oh, tee-hee-hee, I've got to a great bit. Jas's big snogging scene with her "boyfriend".

I'm going to phone Jazzy Spazzy.

Jas answered the phone.

"Jas."

"What?"

"Why are you saying what like that?"

"Like what?"

"Anyway, have you got to your brilliant bit in *Rom and Jule* when your boyfriend climbs into your bedchamber for the night?"

She put the phone down, which is a bit rude.


Ten minutes later

OK, this is the summary of *Rom and Jule*.

It starts with a bit of fighting between two families. When I say families, I mean boys stropping around and so on. Jule is not allowed to do what she wants by her vati because she is only a girl and he will not let her have any fun. (Typico.)

However, her family throws a party and Rom gatecrashes it with his mates. I am in this bit and I go along with Rom to party and dancey aroundy like ye fool.

Which actually might be a bit of a larf.

I will note down some suggestions for Miss Wilson for my interpretation of my part (oo-er).

My dance note is: Perhaps Scottish dancing here.

After the party there is a bit more fighting.

Note for Miss Wilson: Plenty of tomato ketchup here.

Then I have my big death scene and I die telling that hilarious world-renowned joke, "Ask for me tomorrow and you shall find me a grave man."

Do you get it? Do you see?

Die... grave... ?

Oh, it's a side-splitter.

And thankfully, that is it for me. I can scamper off backstage.

To play around with the backstage lads (oo-er).

If the play gets that far that is.

Because I tell you this for free, if Dave the Laugh and his mates have anything to do with building the scenery, the balcony scene is bound to quite literally bring the house down.

Five minutes later

Anyway, what happens next after I die? Not that I care because I won't be watching.

♡ 187

Hmmm.

Rom and Jule spend the night together getting up to hanky panky and possibly rudey-dudeys. We will never know because it's all in some sort of verse about the moon and so on.

Then they get married secretly.

Note for Miss Wilson: Papier mâché heads can be "happening" and "now". They have the "Bingo!" factor.

As a v. good plan, Jule goes to the vicar to ask for help and advice. (The vicar is not "Call me Arnold" but for all the use he is, he should be called "Call me Arnold".)

Back on stage, Jule pretends to take poison and die, Rom finds her, thinks she's dead so he commits suicide. She wakes up and stabs herself.

Note: Plenty of blood capsules and liver here.

The end.

It's a lovely, cheery little tale.

For the sake of the audience, I must make my comedy fight scenes last as long as possible.

Maybe I could accidentally kill Jule's comedy puppet dog.

Note here for Miss Wilson: Comedy dog gets it.

**ll:OO p.m.**

I heard Mum come in from her workshop. Uh-oh.

Dad called out, "Hello, Connie."

But she is not talking to him so... there was a bit of silence and then she said, "Bob, would you run me a bath with some rose oil in it and get me a cold glass of wine, please?"

What? Yes, in your dreams, Madame Zara.

**Ten minutes later**

He's doing it. How amazing.

Surely just doing something with a boiled egg and a coloured scarf doesn't make Dad turn into, erm... unDad.

## Slim's snogging lecture

## Thursday September 29th
French

As they probably say in *la belle France*, *qu'est-ce que c'est le point of France?*

3:00 p.m.
Read-through

Had our first proper read-through of *Rom and Jule*.

Our star-studded cast features:

Me as Merc-lurk-io

Miss Prissy Knickers (Jas) as Jule

Ellen as Tybalt (or something, what do you think... oh, am I the page as well or something?)

Rosie in a *tour de force* and also possibly a beard, as the Nurse.

The octopus in the ointment is, of course, waiting for Ms No Forehead to come and be Rom.

Then Miss Wilson said, "I'm afraid Lindsay cannot be at the read-through today. She has to go for an interview for college."

We all pretended to cry and shouted out, "Ah prithee, lackaday."

"Have you seen my tights?"

"Gadzooks!"

And so on for a while.

As Nauseating P. Green was only "townspeople", she read the Rom part.

She was so excited her glasses steamed up.

I said to Jas, "You lucky, lucky tart."

But Jas shoved me away.

She always takes these things soooo seriously. And I think she really does believe that it is the story of her and Hunky.

Halfway through it was complete chaos with Rosie shouting, "Am I on? Shall I wear my Nurse's beard?"

And Jas was saying stuff like, "But what is my motivation here? Why would I suddenly go across to the balcony window? Perhaps I heard a night owl?"

Absolute wubbish stuff. Jas insists on getting owls in everything. I just wanted to get to the fighting bit. I said to Miss Wilson, "Have you got the swords yet?"

And she dithered about, saying ridiculous stuff like, "Perhaps for now you could use a pointed finger."

Is she mad?

Yes is the answer you are searching (not very far) for.

I said to Miss Wilson, "May I just illustrate my point vis-à-vis the ultimate crapnosity of trying to have a sword fight with a pointed finger?"

I did the bit where we have the fisticuffs and Tybalt stabs me (Merc-lurk-io) to death.

I put my finger up and said, "Tybalt, you rat catcher! Will you walk?"

Which is my fave bit actually.

Then Ellen (as Tybaltio) says, "I am for you", or in Ellen's case, "Er, is it this bit or something, do I, is it for..."

I said, "Ellen, just say 'I am for you' and then fight me to the death."

Bloody hopeless.

Ellen came shuffling over, pointing her finger at me. Ooooh, scary. I jabbed my finger at her and she stuck her finger in my waist. Which I didn't notice actually, until I said, "Come on, get on with it. Stab me to death with your index finger."

And she said, "I, er, I just did."

I looked at Miss Wilson and said, "Do you see? We need swords and plenty of them, and blood. And maybe a bit of old liver. Have you got blood bags?"

Rosie said, "I can make severed fingers out of sausages."

At which point a strange woman came in. In really bright clothes.

Miss Wilson was all over her like a rash. Bobbing like a bobbing thing.

"Oh, girls, girls, this is Miriam. She has come to improvise with us this morning. She has trained with *Le Coq*."

We just about managed to get ourselves under control. I thought Rosie might have to go to the school nurse she was laughing so much.

Nauseating P. Green was the only one who looked a bit puzzled. She was blinking and saying, "What is so funny?"

Rosie said, "I don't think P. Green understands how vair *amusant* a grown-up saying she has trained with *Le Coq* is. I don't think she gets it."

I said, "She wouldn't get it if it came in a big bag labelled 'IT'."

And I am not wrong.

Twenty minutes later

If we thought Miss Wilson was odd, Miriam took the biscuit odd-wise. She was mega odd. And a half.

She was dressed mostly in coloured scarves, with two or three round her head and she wore big shoes and kept falling over things.

Rosie said, "Is Miriam breaking those shoes in for a clown?"

Sadly, Miriam WAS a clown.

We weren't allowed to just say our boring old lines. We had to do mime and clown gestures.

We had to find our inner clown.

4:00 p.m.

Still, it passes the time.

Thank God, the final bell.

As we slouched off to the cloakroom, I said to the gang, "I'm bloody exhausted, and I will tell you this for free, I am not wearing tights and a big red nose."

Jools said, "She won't really make us wear the noses, will she? I thought we were just wearing them to please Mad Miriam."

Jas said, "Actually, I found it quite liberating doing the clowning. I found a different part of Juliet, sort of more playful. She is just a teenager after all. Like us."

We all looked at her.

I said, "She is five hundred and fifty years old."

Jas was ready to do storming off in the huffmobile when I said, "Actually, you might be right, Jas. If you and your boyfriend, Wet Lindsay, wear clown noses, that would put proper snogging out of the question. *Voilà*! Bob *est l'oncle*!!"

**4:05 p.m.**

Things are hotting up in the Miss Wilson and Rudi Kamyer department. They walked out of the school gates together tonight. Miss Wilson looked like she was showing him her inner clown. Bobbing her head around like a demented pigeon. Rudi took off his glasses and cleaned them with his scarf. That is how vair vair excited he was.

Luckily, it's German tomorrow.


**Three minutes later**

Crikey, Masimo is at the gates again! Back to the bloody loo for me for glamour work.


**6:00 p.m.**

They are awfully demonstrative, the Pizza-a-gogo types.

And also not inhibited.

When he saw me, the Luuurve God actually came through the school gates into the playground. And then he snogged me among the milling girls. Who were all squeaking and shrieking like wild geese.

It seems a bit sort of pervy snogging someone in the school playground.

I don't know why.

I don't associate Sex Gods with school.

Or anything to do with rudey-dudey or snoggy-poos.

In fact, when we had so-called "Sex Education" with someone called Mrs Tampax (probably), I had my fingers in my ears and was humming.

It's just not right...

The Ace Gang sloped off and Masimo took me home on his scooter.

**7:00 p.m.**
**In my private boudoir of luuurve**
He has given me a little locket.

Crikey.

It's a heart with a photo of him inside.

He's on a beach in his jeans and he doesn't have a top on.

I must never ever ever mention this to Dave the Laugh.

I can imagine what he will say.

Anyway, shut up. I am not imagining what he will say.

**10:00 p.m.**
The Luuurve God says he will miss me when he goes to

♡ 197

Lunnern town this weekend. But a little break doesn't hurt anyone I say.

### Two minutes later

I seem to be the only one who does say it though. The rest of the gang are practically glued to their boyfriends. What happened to the one for all and one for one and all in all fandango?

### Four minutes later

I heard Mum call out to Dad, "Bob, would you put a hot-water bottle in bed for me? And a cup of hot chocolate would be lovely. Thank you."

I don't know what is going on with Mum and Dad, but it's weird.

Mum keeps asking Dad to do things, and he keeps doing them.

### Two minutes later

Unfortunately, she hasn't said, "Hand over your money and make your way to Europe."

I have pinned a photo of the wildcats on the shed door

so that Angus can look at them.

He likes it a lot. He stares and stares and then does that silent miaowing thing.

Then he starts shaking.

I can see him through my bedroom window.

I thought it would be a relief for Bum-ty but unfortunately Angus divides his time equally between staring at his photo and budgie staring.

## Friday September 30th

Hurrah. Nearly freedom. Thank you, Baby Jesus, for leading us through another week of pain and tribulation (triple maths and "David Copperpants").

Lurching out of assembly. Which was only bearable because Slim nearly fell up the stairs when she went on to the stage. She so clearly can't see where her feet are.

Wet Lindsay came up to me after assembly and said, "Nicolson, the headmistress wants to see you in her office, now."

What had I done?

What?

I knocked on Slim's door and she said, "Come."

Oh God.

### Ten minutes later
One of the most embarrassing things in the history of embarrassmentosity has happened.

It was so horrific. I may have to go lie down in the loos.

### Two minutes later
Hawkeye was taking Geoggers and when I walked in late, she said, "So pleased you managed to fit us into your busy schedule, Georgia. Sit down and treat us to your description of the formation of an oxbow lake."

Oh God.

### Break
The Ace Gang all crowded round me at break going, "What happened?"

"Did the clown lady complain?"

Rosie said, "Yes, did she tell that we laughed at *Le Coq*?"

I looked at her.

I said, "She talked about snogging."

Rosie opened her eyes wide.

"Oh my God."

I said, "Slim has given me a sex lecture."

The Ace Gang went, "Nooooo."

"Oh yes. An onion bhaji has talked to me about snogging."

All the Ace Gang went, "Erlack, that is soooo disgusting."

Rosie said, "Phone the police now."

Oh, I feel dirty.

Rosie said, "Did she actually say, 'What number have you got up to on the Snogging Scale?' "

"No, thank God. It was mostly 'inappropriate behaviour in front of the younger girls... Running before I could walk... Saving yourself for the right young man... All in good time'. In fact, a quick summary would be, 'Blah blah blah rave on rave on. Tremble tremble... Have some pride and dignity'."

Rosie said, "What she means really is, don't tart around so much."

"Thank you for that, Rosie."

Lunchtime
I feel besmirched.

I asked Miss Stamp if I could have a shower even though we haven't had games today. She said, "Go on then, but I'm coming to keep an eye on you."

Bloody hell, this place is quite literally like *Prisoner Cell Block H.*

**Two hours later**
How dare Slim talk about my private parts.

I don't talk about hers.

I don't even think about hers.

Oh God!!!!

I just have done!!!

**Last lesson of the week and fortunately it's German**
I may even get a light snooze in before home time.

I said that to the gang.

"I am *absolutement* full of exhaustosity. I feel like I have been through the mangle of luuurve."

Which I have.

Rosie has been reading her *German for Fools* book again.

She said to me, "Prat is *Volltrotte!*"

It's a *sehr* musical language.

Basoomas in German is *mopse.*

As the bell rang, Rosie leaped up and did comedy beard work.

She had her beard underneath her desk and she was pretending to beat it off her face and yelling, "Herr Kamyer, Herr Kamyer, *ich glaub mich knutscht ein* Hamster!!!"

Herr Kamyer blinked through his glasses and then said very quickly, "*Guten Abend.*"

And walked out quickly.

I said, "What did you say?"

And Rosie said, "I think a hamster is snogging me."

**4:10 p.m.**

I was quite relieved when I got to the school gates and there was no sign of the Luuurve God. Slim is sure to be on snogging alert somewhere, probably with binoculars. She could quite easily hide them about her person and you would never know.

**4:20 p.m.**

As we walked along as a gang, it was nice and jolly.

And a relief to be away from Stalag 14.

And just to have the weekend stretching before me.

No one has got a proper plan for the weekend as there is no gig or anything, but we are going to have a ringaround. I feel really happy and free. I don't know why.

Rosie said, "*Rom and Jule* could do with a bit of livening up, couldn't it? Music wise? Couldn't we ask Miss Wilson if we could have a song or two? Cheer things up a bit in among the suicide and fighting?"

Hmmmm.

### Four minutes later

We are all skipping along (yes, I do mean skipping along) singing songs from *The Sound of Music*. It was that ye olde Shakespearean classic, "The hills are alive with the sound of tights, with tights I have worn for a thousand years"!!!!!

We were just all singing, "I go to the hills when my tights are loneleee..." when Dave and the lads leaped out from behind a tree.

I was so flustered I nearly fell over.

When I got my breath back, I said, "Have you been following us?"

Dave said, "Yes."

I said, "Well that's not nice, is it?"

Dave said, "Yes. It is."

"No, it's not."

"It is. I particularly noticed your basoomas wiggling about when you were skipping."

"That's disgusting."

"I liked it."

"Don't you feel ashamed, sneaking about and so on?"

"*Nein, ich* feel *gut!*"

I said, "I think you will find you are a bit of a *Volltrotte*."

He said, "*Ach, Scheissenhausen!*"

He does make me laugh.

## Five minutes later

We all lolloped along together. The lads were in top moods because of a *coup d'état* they had done at school. They had drawn a massive boy's trouser snake on the playing field with weedkiller.

They'd done it under cover of playing footie and then just waited for it to emerge.

Dave said, "Top-class group work."

I very nearly told them about my "snogging lecture" from

Slim, but I didn't want to talk about the Luuurve God in front of Dave the Laugh.

I did tell him about Mad Miriam and how we had had to find our inner clown.

Dave said, "Has your inner clown got a Horn?"

At the bottom of the hill everyone else peeled off to go home. The casual plan is to go to the cinema tomorrow eves. Dave walked along with me. He pushed me in the arm and loosened his tie and smiled at me.

"Long time since we did this, isn't it, Kittykat? You're too frightened of the call of my Magnetic Horn to be alone with me, aren't you?"

I said, "Er, Dave, I am not frightened of your Magnetic Horn and that is *le* fact."

He said, "You are."

"I'm not."

"You are."

"I'm not and just repeating something doesn't make it an argument."

"It does."

"It does not... hang on a minute, we're doing it again. Stop it..."

There was a silence then he said, "No, you stop it."

He is soooo annoying. Funny though.

We didn't talk about the Luuurve God or Emma, although I half expected her to come running up behind us with some warm milk for Dave or something. Is that what happens to girls around boys – they just turn into zombie girls?

Somebody should try telling my mum that she is supposed to be a man-pleaser. She asked Dad to polish her shoes last night. And he did! What is all that about?

When we reached my turn-off, Dave said, "So what are you up to tomorrow night?"

I said, "Well, I... erm, the rest of them want to go to the cinema, but you know... it'll be like Snog Central and... I..."

He looked at me with his crinkly eyes.

"And your girlfriend is not around."

I said, "Oy... but, well, yes, I guess."

There was a moment's pause and then Dave said, "Well, I'll be on my jacksie as well, so maybe see you there. S'laters."

Blimey.

When I got to my house, Masimo was sitting outside on his scooter chatting to Mum and Libby! Libby had got his spare helmet on, so was essentially a helmet on a pair of legs. I could hear her laughing inside the helmet.

Five minutes later

Why doesn't Mum go in with Libby? I keep raising my eyebrows and looking at her in a meaningful way, but she doesn't know what I mean.

Masimo has put his arms around me, and I am half sitting on his knee. I feel weird in front of my mum.

Oh joy unbounded, Oscar is lurking about. Does he really think that wearing a baseball cap backwards is going to get him a girlfriend? Also, when he jumped over his gate, he caught his shoe in his falling-down jeans fiasco and head-dived into his dad's perennials (quite literally oo-er).

Sad really.

Also, I can't help noticing, I am in my school uniform. This is not the air of sophisticosity I am aiming for.

Also, even though nothing was going on with Dave the Laugh, except just matewise, I couldn't help thinking what would have happened if the Luuurve God had seen us skipping along together. Talking about Dave's Magnetic Horn.

Dave seemed more like Dave the Laugh again. He hadn't

shown any sign of numptiness, which is good.

Not that I care really, but well, you know.

Don't you? I hope you do because I certainly don't.

As my brain burbled merrily on by itself, Masimo said, "*Cara*, I must go. We are driving, now, for London. I am missing you. *Bellissima* Georgia." And he kissed me on the lips. In front of my mother. Dear God.

Mum said, "How beautiful. See you when you get back and good luck with everything."

Then Masimo went and gave her two kisses on either cheek. He said, "*Bella mama.*"

My mother practically collapsed on the spot. Then she laughed like a fool and said, "Ooohhh."

The romantic mood was spoiled a bit by the complete fandango of getting the spare helmet off Libby. First of all she said, "No, I laaaaaike it. It's mine."

And ran off to hide.

Of course, being a helmet on legs doesn't make it easy to hide. Nor does the fact that she thinks just standing very still behind a small tree makes her invisible. When I went and got her, she kicked my leg and said, "Shhhh, Gingey, I am hiding, you bad boy."

I lured her out of it by the Jammy Dodger bribe. She couldn't eat them with the helmet on, but I also had to promise to read her *Heidi*. AGAIN!!!

Mum tried to help by suggesting I read something called *The Magic Faraway Tree* by Enid Blyton.

At least it's trees instead of cheese.

### Reading The Magic Faraway Tree
### Twenty minutes later

Why do they let impressionable children read this sort of thing? It has even freaked Libby out because it is so insane. There is some bloke called Moonface in it. And he has got a moonface. Literally. Isn't that a bit moon-ist?

### In my bedroom

It's odd having someone really like you. Am I that brilliant? Maybe all Pizza-a-gogo boys are like Masimo.

Hang on a minute, Rom is a Pizza-a-gogo type. It's all fitting together now. Rom only snogged Jule once before he shinned up her drainpipe (oo-er) and then he married her and committed suicide.

Perhaps all Pizza-a-gogo boys are the same.

## Two minutes later

If I hear a scrabbling noise outside my bedroom window one night, it might not be Angus dragging some half-eaten cockroach for me to look at. It might be Masimo wanting a midnight wedding.

Crikey. I've already got a locket.

## 8:30 p.m.

Masimo phoned just before he set off.

He said, "Miss Georgia, will you wait for me?"

I was thinking, blimey, mate, it's only a day and a half. But I said yes.

I hadn't really thought about it before, but I suppose if he did go on tour, we might not see each other all the time.

And there would be loads of girls around him.

But he is not a red-bottomed Hornmeister, is he?

The question is... am I?

## Two minutes later

No, I am most certainly not. I am the girlfriend of a Luuurve God and that is the end of the story.

Oh yes, I have dabbled in the cakeshop of life, but those days are well and truly over now.

I have settled for an Italian fancy. And I am not a jam tart.

### Three minutes later

What did Dave the Laugh mean when he said he would be on his jacksie?

### Four minutes later

I phoned Jas.

"Jas?"

"Hmmm."

"Are you going to deffo go to the cinema?"

"Yes, I think so. The only thing is, if Tom has got some special stones he was talking about, then we would put them in the aquarium."

"Right, so it's either the cinema or putting stones in a tank. I see. Erm, Jas, is, erm, are, Dave the Laugh and Emma going?"

"Why?"

"It's just a question, Jas."

"I know, but it's nothing to do with you pretending I fancy Dave the Laugh, is it?"

"You have a vair suspicious nature; it's sad."

"Well, why are you asking me? Anyway, Emma has gone on a sketching weekend with her art teacher, so she won't be there."

### In my room

The vair weird thing was that I was sort of looking forward to going to the cinema now.

What was all that about?

### Half an hour later

Just for the crack of being with your mates.

That's all.

You know, relaxing and watching a film with your mates.

Simple, uncomplicated stuff.

# Sven finds his inner woman (unfortunately)

## Saturday October 1st

**9:00 a.m.**

Something's vair vair wrong. It's so quiet.

What is so weird?

**9:10 a.m.**

I know what it is. No one has come barging into my room making me do stuff.

Also, I am in my bed, by myself.

No cats chewing my hair.

No Libby dancing around in suspiciously bulging pongie pants

One minute later

No, I tell a lie, I am not alone. I have got Mr Potato Head with me. I didn't realise at first because he has got his sock "nightdress" on...

Urgh, Mr Potato Head is going a bit green.

I can't believe I nearly snogged him when I had snogging withdrawal.

I don't fancy him half so much now he is losing his looks!!!!

Hahahahahahaha.

Shut up.

Why is it so quiet though?

Oh, I thought it was too good to be true. I can hear the distinct approach of some portly bloke lumbering up the stairs to my b.o.l. (boudoir of luuurve). It will be Vati larging in with some ludicrous scheme to go and look around some pie factory somewhere. For hints on how to get even larger in the botty department.

The steps stopped outside my door and there was a knock.

What?

Then Vati said from outside the door, "Georgia, I have

brought you a cup of tea. Your mum said you would like one. May I bring it in for you?"

What was this? It must be some plan of his to get me to do something horrific, like come and watch him play "football" with his mates. Twenty-two out-of-condition men lumbering around a pitch for twenty minutes before most of them are sent off for fighting. (Or, as happened when I last went, Uncle Eddie got sent off for having a fag and a beer with the goalkeeper. During the game.)

### Two minutes later
I said, "You can come in with the tea as long as you just leave it and don't say anything."

### Three minutes later
Am I suddenly living in *Wind in the Willows* and Dad is kindly old Badger? He didn't say anything to me, just put the tea down and smiled at me and went away.

It must be some sort of trick to lull me into a false sense of security.

He was even almost normally dressed. In a proper jumper and trousers.

Not leatherette or anything.

Crikey.

## Fifteen minutes later

This is the life, just lying here letting my pores breathe.

I wonder if I should start to cleanse and tone?

Also I must remember to replenish my pouch. I've gone through all my lip gloss in the last few days because of all the unexpected popping up that has been going on. Vis-à-vis the Luuurve God.

He'll be in Lunnern now hanging around with the Chelsea set.

Do I want it to go well or not?

What do management people do anyway?

## Five minutes later

At least I have got my locket.

My precious locket of my beloved Luuurve God.

Where is my locket by the way?

## Fourteen minutes later

I forgot I had put it in my pouch, in case I was body-searched on the way out of Stalag 14 for smiling or something.

I am going to phone Jas and see if she is coming tonight. And make her come anyway.

### Downstairs

There is quiet music playing from the bathroom. As I picked up the phone, Dad came by with another cup of tea. He'll probably throw it over me and start yelling about the phone bill.

But he just smiled and said, "Good morning; sleep well?" and knocked on the bathroom door.

Mum said, "Come."

And Dad shuffled in with the tea.

Something really weird was going on. Mum was hardly ever out of the bath and Dad hadn't gone ballistic in hours.

Has he turned into a Stepford Dad?

### One minute later

Jas answered the phone.

Before I could say anything she started going, "Guess what, guess what's the bestiest thing ever!!"

Oh, what did that mean? The best thing on Planet Jas could be anything.

I said, "Something to do with a new strain of vole poo? You've got a stuffed barn owl? No, no, don't tell me. Your pants have a new all-weather stretch gusset?"

She was going, "Nope, nope, you will never guess, it's so soooooo bestie!"

I said, "Jas, if it's anything to do with the newts getting a helter skelter I don't think I can bear the excitement."

She was too excited to notice my amusingnosity. She just burbled on. "The *Rom and Jule* thing, it's all, well... it's all fabby and marv. In fact, it's a miracle."

"I think you will find it's a tragedy, unless Miss Wilson has rewritten the ending so that Jule wakes up in time and finds her inner clown, with hilarious consequences."

Jas was talking over the top of me.

"Tom just told me, she's got to take a uni bursary exam. She can't be in it!!"

"Who?"

"Wet Lindsay!!!!"

Oh, joy unbounded.

Mind you, it would have been vair amusing to see Jas snogging Wet Lindsay. In an horrific, road crash sort of way.

Also Radio Jas tells me that there has been a change of plan cinema experience wise. I can't decide if it is good or bad.

Or a combo of good and bad. Goba. Or maybe even bago. Depending on how you look at it. Shut up, brain.

Rosie's parents have gone away for the night and she is planning on having the cinema experience at her place.

Hmmmmm.

I phoned her and said, "When you say 'cinema experience', what exactly do you mean by that?"

She said, "You know what I mean, my little pally. All of us in the dark, snogging and eating popcorn."

I said, "Yes, but the added mystery ingredient in the usual 'cinema experience' is that there is a film on."

Rosie assures me that there will be a film on, a "special" film. But she won't tell me what it is as she wants it to be a "lovely surprise".

Now I am frightened.

And I can't quite be sure that Dave the Laugh will be

there. And I can't ask anyone to check. If I ask Radio Jas and say, "Please will you not tell anyone I am asking, just use subtlenosity," Dave would be on the blower within five minutes saying, "Why do you want me to come to the cinema experience? Can't you resist my Magnetic Horn?"

What shall I do if he isn't there? I will be the goosegog fool of all time. But I can't just leave if he's not there because otherwise that looks like I really meant to see him.

And then the cat would be out of the bag.

Racing down the hill with the bag over its head.

Why is it in the bag anyway?

Speaking of cats, when I went down to the kitchen for a soothing plate of cheesy wotsits to calm my nerves, Angus was playing with his tartan toy mousey.

He was biffing toy mousey with one paw and then biffing him back with the other. Then picking him up by his neck and shaking him. Then he biffed toy mousey really hard and it went under the fridge.

Angus started trying to reach under with his paw. But he couldn't reach. Then he started his croaky miaowing and the looking at me pathetically fiasco.

### Three minutes later

I was chomping away on the cheesies. I must keep my strength up for my maybe goosegogging experience tonight.

### One minute later

Angus was still trying to reach toy mousey and still looking pathetically at me.

### Two minutes later

Oh, I can't stand this.

I lay down on the floor and put my arm under the fridge to try to reach toy mousey. Angus was pressing my bottom with his paw as I was doing it. Sort of encouraging me, I suppose.

### Two minutes later

It's right at the back. I can sort of touch it with my fingers, but I can't reach it to pull it out.

### Two minutes later

I got the washing-up brush and nearly got it.

Oh, bloody hell, it's gone a bit further back.

**Three minutes later**

Just about got it.

Just a centimetre or two more.

**One minute later**

Got it!!!

Stood up. Blimey, I'm a bit dizzy.

I said to Angus, "There you are, now don't…"

He's just biffed it straight back under the fridge.

And started his croaky miaowing and looking thing.

**6:30 p.m.**

When I went back in the kitchen for more cheesy wotsits, Mum was down on the floor scrabbling under the fridge for toy mousey.

I didn't say anything.

**6:45 p.m.**

She's got it out.

**6:46 p.m.**

He's biffed it back under the fridge again.

**7:00 p.m.**

Libby is being taken over to Grandvati's because Mum and Dad are going out on a "date". Which is sad. They even said "date". Erlack.

As I was setting off to Rosie's "cinema experience", Vati was faffing around adjusting his fur steering wheel. I tried to just sneak off past him but he spotted me and said, "Have a nice time, but you won't be having as nice a time as us because your mother and I are off to paint the town red."

I said, "Don't you mean beige?"

And just for a moment I caught sight of my dear old dad, the dad I know and... well, the dad I knew. He went all red and ballistic-looking and started shouting, "You're not bloody funny, and what time will you be in? Because I am telling you this for free..."

Then he sort of stopped himself as Mum came out all tarted up and forced this very scary smile on his face. I watched while he opened the mirthmobile door for her and put Libby in the back.

Then I watched as Libby did a bit of kicking of the car seats and shouting. "Me want Bum-ty, me want Bum-ty!!! Go get her, Big Uggy!!!!"

And Dad went back into the house and came out with Bum-ty in her cage. Bum-ty seems to have less and less feathers. And she has gone off her Trill.

I'm not surprised with the twenty-four-hour cat staring that goes on.

Tonight Angus even managed to get on top of Bum-ty's cage. Even though Dad has fixed it to the light fitting and it's suspended from the ceiling.

Angus must have used the sofa as a launch pad, leaped up the curtains and hurled himself on to the cage from there. In a Devil take the hindmost kat-i-kaze diving episode. It's only because his paws are so huge that he couldn't get them through the bars.

**7:15 p.m.**
Anyway, at last the Swiss Family Mad streaked off at one mile an hour.

Some people live life in the fast lane. My dad lives life in the bus lane.

As I strolled along, I nearly caught up with them. I had to take really tiny steps to avoid walking alongside.

## At Rosie's

Sven answered the door in an usherette's uniform. If you can imagine that. It's not easy, I know. He had a sort of mini-skirt on with platform boots. And a lot of eyeshadow and lippy.

Not expertly applied I have to say.

Sofas and chairs were arranged in front of their big-screen TV and Rosie was in charge of popcorn. I say in charge. What I mean is she was stoking up the popcorn maker, a duck that made popcorn that came shooting out of its beak.

The Ace Gang were all there by the time I arrived. Hons, Jools, Ellen, Mabs and Sophie, all snuggling up to their "boyfriends" already.

It was so crowded, I even wondered if the Little Titches might pop up from behind something. I'm not kidding. I wouldn't be surprised. If they have even a whiff (half a whiff) that Dave the Laugh might be in the area, they would be scampering around trying to get near to him.

Is he in the area though?

Fourteen minutes later

No sign of Dave the Laugh.

Goosegog land was approaching.

Oh God, this was going to be horrific.

Even now it was horrific and the film hadn't even started. The one hilarious moment was when Ellen did the classic bobbing around like a pigeon wondering which side to put her head for the snog.

Maybe I could pretend I had a sudden pressing piddly-diddly scenario and sneak out through the bathroom window.

Just then the doorbell rang. Sven the usherette went to answer it and carried in Dave the Laugh.

Dave said, "I like a big girl."

I didn't say anything. I felt a bit shy actually. And sort of nervy.

Dave got his popcorn and then came and sat down next to me.

I have to say, even though I am not interested in this sort of thing, that he looked, well, quite fit. For a matey-type mate.

The film was the sing-along version of *The Sound of Music*.

No, I am not kidding.

Sven (the usherette) introduced it by saying, "This is a film about the *unter*garments. We are haffing the singing about pants and the lederhosen. Let's groove!"

And then he switched the lights out.

We were plunged into complete darkness. Everyone was going, "Oo-er" and "Phwoooaar" etc. for a bit.

Then, in the darkness, Dave the Laugh said loudly, "Oy, Georgia, is that your hand on my knee, you cheeky, cheeky minx?"

What what???

It turned out to be Sven's hand. Sven was crawling around trying to find the control for the screen.

We sang, we ate popcorn. The film even had the bouncing ball lyrics because it was the sing-alonga one.

It should have been crapnosity personified, but it was not.

And the best thing was that the goosegog factor was vair low because no one really had any time for snogging.

My ribs really, really did hurt from laughing so much.

Sometimes we had reversed the film so that we could get the song again. We sang them all:

"The hills are alive with the sound of pants."

"Idlepants", as I have said many, many times, is one of my all-time hits.

Rosie said, "I am deffo going to have songs from *The Sound of Music* at my Viking wedding. The Vikings love a bit of yodelling."

It was after midnight before we came out. When we got to the end of Rosie's road, the rest of them walked off because they all lived in the same direction. They were yelling, "Pants for the memory!"

"*Guten Nacht, Volltrotte!*"

"*Abscheidskuss* all round!"

Till there was only Dave and me left.

It was a lovely soft night and as we walked along, I felt all warm and yummy inside.

Dave said, "I'll walk back along your way in case you are attacked by voles."

I said, "Fanks."

We didn't link up or anything and walked a bit apart. You know, in a sort of matey way. I think.

Then Dave said, "Well, I don't know what you think, missus, but I thought that was quite literally a hoot and a half. I thought your yodelling in 'The lonely goatherd' was, well, good is not the word."

I said, "Oy, mate, I have practised yodelling for weeks. Libby makes me read *Heidi* at least four times a day."

As we got near my house, Dave said, "Ah well, better say *Auf Wiedersehen,* pet."

And we both stood looking at each other in the half light.

He has got the most dreamy eyes. I don't know what it is, but I always feel like I could look at him for ages and ages. (Not in an Angus and Gordy looking at Bum-ty way.)

I don't know how much time went by because for once my brain froze.

I sort of felt like Baby Jesus, all full of love.

Dave put his hand on my face and just gently stroked it.

Then he traced his finger around my mouth.

Oh no, stop puckering!!!

He looked down at me still with his finger on my lips and said, "I don't know what it is about you, Kittykat, but for me you are the most beautiful girl in the world."

Then he kissed me, just a little kiss.

I sort of reached up to kiss him back, but he stepped back then and pulled his coat collar up.

He breathed in really deeply and then cleared his throat and said, "Hmmm, that was a bit unexpected... but anyway, dig you later."

I didn't know what to say. Or do.

I just stood there.

I wanted to do all sorts of things. Grab him, run away, laugh uncontrollably. Snog, go to the loo, do a bit of the flame dance. I don't know!!!! Who is in control here?

As I dithered around, he walked off home.

When I got in, Mum and Dad were still up. And they weren't alone. Uncle Eddie was there. He's just "popped" by after a baldy-o-gram night. He hasn't been round much since the undercrackers at midnight scenario. Dad said they were "letting things cool down" neighbourwise.

I said, "Why, are you pretending that you and Uncle Eddie are not gay?"

Anyway, sadly, they seem to be together again.

As I tried to scamper upstairs, Uncle Eddie said, "This is one for you, Georgia. A man goes to the doctor and says, 'I keep thinking I'm a cartoon character. One day I'm Mickey Mouse, this morning I was convinced I was Bambi.' And the doctor says, 'It sounds to me like you're having Disney spells.'"

I looked at him as he rocked and hooted with laughter, going, "Do you see??? Do you see... Disney spells!!!"

What is the point of Uncle Eddie?

### In bed
### 1:00 a.m.
Blimey.

Well, the cinema experience turned out to be a hoot and a half. The laughter, the pants, the yodelling.

### One minute later
The nearly accidentally snogging Dave the Laugh AGAIN!!!

What in the name of arse is going on?

### Two minutes later
What about Masimo?

I think I may have a touch of guiltosity.

### Two minutes later
Although I don't know why I should have guiltosity – I haven't really done anything wrong as such. Involuntary puckering is not a capital offence.

### One minute later

In fact, I will probably mention it in a light-hearted way to the Luuurve God.

You know, tell him what larks we had at the "cinema experience".

### Two minutes later

Although explaining the "Idlepants" thing might take the rest of my life, given that I can't even say "What time is it?" in Italian.

Oh, I am just a crazy, mixed-up kid!!! It's not fair. If you look at the relativitosity of time and pretend that my life is a big clock... and I'm at three o'clock, it's only about five minutes since I first learned to do my shoes up at kindergarten. And so how come I am supposed to be an expert at relationships???

I only started snogging last year. (Half past two.)

Shut up about the clock fiasco!!!!

I didn't even have any basoomas eighteen months ago... (i.e. quarter to one... shut up, shut up, brain!!!).

I was practically just a nose on legs.

### Two minutes later

OOOhhh. I'm never going to be able to go to sleep now.

I wonder if Dave is feeling the same.

I hope he is because it's his fault. He snogged me. I only did accidental puckering up.

It was him who said I was beautiful.

Am I?

Had a look in the mirror.

Erm, well, as I said, I have sort of grown into my nose, but I don't exactly as such look like a supermodel.

Perhaps boys like all sorts of girls not just supermodelly types.

Dad likes Mum, for instance, and does not think she looks like a mad prostitute.

In fact, he is very bloody keen on her these days.

I wonder if she is putting something in his food?

### Five minutes later

I'm going to count sheep to get to sleep.

### Three minutes later

Oh buggeration, the sheep keep changing into Masimo, and

then Dave, and then Robbie, and then Masimo and then two Daves. And then Dave with a clown nose on, leaping over the fence. And then Masimo with a handbag. Then Dave and Masimo fighting and leaping over the fence.

I will never ever sleep again. I zzzzzzzzzzzzzzzzzzzzzz.

# I may have a slight fence burn

## Sunday October 2nd

Yipppeee we are going to take Angus to the kittykat park!

Mum has gone ballistic because Angus was going on and on, miaowing and rubbing round her legs. Tripping her up when she tried to walk anywhere. He's had his food so she put some water down for him in his bowl. He looked at it and then instead of lapping it up, he leaped in it and splashed it all over the floor and her.

She tried to chuck him out, but he ran off into the front room and he's managed to get himself into the back of the armchair.

She said, "He's not coming with us."

I said, "Mum, he's excited. He is hearing the call of the wild."

She said, "Go and get his lead. I'm putting my gardening gloves on."

We eventually got Angus out of the armchair and on his lead. It was all going quite well until he had a spontaneous spaz attack and wound himself round and round my legs...

When Pippy turned up in her car, Mum said to Dad, "You don't mind not coming, do you, Bob? Perhaps you could fix the shed roof this afternoon. I would be so thrilled if you did."

I looked at her in an "are you mad" way.

As if Dad will agree to that. The last time he fixed a ceiling, he went into the attic to have a look, walked in between the rafters and now his big fat footprints are there for ever.

To my absolute amazement, he gave her a big kiss on the mouth (oh, dear God) and said, "All right, my queen. Missing you already."

As we got in the car, I said to Mum, "Is Dad on drugs?"

And Mum said, "No, but the whole thing I have learned from Madame Betty is..."

I said, "Mum, can I just stop you there. If this is anything to do with boiled eggs and so on, I would rather not know."

She didn't take any notice of me, but just went on chatting to Pippy about stuff they had learned in their stupid workshop thingy.

I was trying not to listen because it was making me feel a bit queasy. Stuff about thinking you are the sexiest woman alive etc. Telling yourself how gorgeous you are.

On and bloody on.

When Mum said, "Next week we are doing how to release your inner lushiousness," I had to stuff two bits of scrumpled-up paper handkerchief in my ears.

### Wild Park!!!

Angus luuurved his wild cousins. The wildcat ladeeez luuurved Angus too, the little furry minxes, laying on their tum tums with their girlie parts flying free.

He really howled when we finally managed to get him away.

To cheer him up because he was still yowling and bonking about in the car, I sang "Wild Thing" to him.

I even improvised a little kittykat disco inferno dance.

And I did the paw actions for him.

He let me work his paws for a bit before he started spitting.

## Home

Dad had hit himself with the hammer, and also the door of the shed had fallen off. So an excellent result DIY-wise.

He was in a foul mood when we got in.

I thought it was too good to last.

It was a bit of a relief to see the Portly One back to normal. He was vati-ing around, moaning and limping. Which is ironic, seeing as he had hit his thumb with the hammer.

## Bobo time

Libbs is still at Grandvati's so I am going to enjoy my bed. Just the luxury of lying on it, without something hideous sticking in my back. Or Libby farting loudly all night.

Anyway, I've got to get myself in the right frame of mind to welcome back my Luuurve God.

I wonder what time he will be back?

He'll probably call me tomorrow.

I'd better check on my loveliness.

Maybe I should have an overnight egg-yolk face pack?

## Two minutes later

No, maybe not. The last time I did I thought that my face had gone paralysed in the night.

Anyway, according to Dave the Laugh, I am beauty personified just as I am.

Which is handy.

I wonder why he said that to me?

The most beautiful girl thing.

Was it a joke?

Why weren't we laughing?

Anyway, shut up, brain.

## Going upstairs

I said, "Goodnight, Mater and Pater. Please keep the noise down."

Dad said, "Oh, by the way, that Italian boy phoned. Masimo, is it? He says to tell you that he is back and he will see you tomorrow. And to think of him and put your hand on your locket. I told him that was going too far."

I said, "Dad, I hate you."

**Midnight**

Masimo is back.

That's fab, isn't it?

I thought Dave might have rung. You know, just for a matey chat. But he didn't. I expect Emma is back and he'll be, you know, seeing her. Or something. Which is fine by me.

# Monday October 3rd

Miss Wilson brought in the puppet dog for Jas. It is hilariously crap. And it is a glove puppet. It doesn't even look like a dog. I think it is a bear. Jas was supposed to work her own dog. She got into a terrible state in the balcony scene.

Miss Wilson suggested that the puppet dog "senses" that Rom is down below in the garden. She said to Jas, "When you, Juliet, say, 'Romeo, Romeo, whyfore art thou, Romeo,' the little faithful dog could bark..."

I said, "Erm, just as a matter of interest, Miss Wilson... wherefore art Romeo?"

Miss Wilson said, "Yes, well..."

I said, "Couldn't the dog double up as Romeo? I think that would be great. Try it, Jas. Get the doggie to say some of Rom's bits."

Jas was getting vair vair red indeedy. She was revving up the huffmobile, big time.

She said to me, "Georgia, shut up about Romeo being the doggy."

I said to her, "I am only trying to help things go with a swing, aren't I?"

### Two minutes later

Miss Wilson announced the new Rom.

And the surprise news is that it's going to be... Melanie Griffiths.

She's a nice girl, Melanie, but she really has got ginormous basoomas.

I said to Rosie, "I don't fancy her chances of climbing up the balcony and not toppling over."

Possibly taking out several villagers on her way down.

But it's not really my prob, as I am dead by about page six.

Frankly, it's not really worth putting the tights on for.

## Ten minutes later

Jas was on the edge of a nervy b. trying to do the barking and tail-waggling thing for the doggy and being Juliet as well.

In the end, she threw the glove puppet to the floor and burst into tears.

## Ten minutes later

It's a dream come true for Nauseating P. Green because she is doubling up as townspeople and doggie. As I say, it's a dream come true for her, but not for anyone else. It's very hard to concentrate on her dog work, as immediately behind the dog is her not unlarge loomy face with huge glasses on it.

Miss Wilson looked a bit worried when Nauseating P. Green suggested an improvised "fetch the stick" moment.

I said to the gang, "Pamela will be doing method acting. She will almost certainly be sleeping in a dog basket tonight."

Jas is not amused of course.

Rom and Jule, otherwise known as Mrs Grumpy Knickers and Melanie, didn't do the kissy kissy bit. Actually, costumewise, there really is going to have to be quite a bit of strapping down. Otherwise Rom won't be able to get near enough to Jule to snog her.

Twelve minutes later

At last we got to the good bit. My fighting bit.

Miss Wilson said, "I was chatting with, erm, Herr Kamyer..."

We all went, "Oh, yes..." And winking and so on. Miss Wilson bobbed madly about.

"Yes, and by a stroke of good fortune, Herr Kamyer did *épée* as a young man. Competitively."

Rosie said, "Miss Wilson, why are you telling us about Herr Kamyer going to the piddly-diddly department?"

Miss Wilson looked completely baffled (no change there then). She said, "I don't understand..."

Rosie said, "You said Herr Kamyer did a pee as a young man. Competitively."

Miss Wilson started giggling like a goose.

"Oh, oh, I see... no, no, I said EPEE... it's a form of swordfighting."

Good Lord.

So Herr Kamyer is going to teach us to swordfight.

We may as well book the hospital now.

## Ten minutes later

Hurrrahhhhhhh! God Bless King Harry and gadzooks etc.

Jas has perked up again now she doesn't have to do any parking.

Or have Wet Lindsay as her boyfriend.

Maybe everything is going to be OK.

We've got the lads coming in for the first tech run-through this week. Wait till Dave the Laugh hears that Melanie Griffiths is going to be Rom.

## Lunchtime

Lolling about in the fives court.

Wet Lindsay and ADM came lurking over just looking at us. What are they looking at?

Octopussy called over to Jas, "Sorry about the play, Jas, but I've just got so much to do, the university thing and now the band going off to live in London."

What? What did she know about the band?

Then she went on talking to ADM. But loud enough for us to hear every word.

She said, "Robbie was so pleased to see me when I popped round last night. It's like he'd been away for months. And he is so cool at snogging. I had a boyfriend before him who was so inexperienced he didn't even know where to put his hands."

I said to Rosie, "I could have told him where to put his hands – round her throat until her goggly eyes popped out. Hell's teeth, she is such a smug bucket."

Jools said, "Did you know they were moving to London?"

No I didn't is the answer.

Wet Lindsay was still going on. I'm sure for my benefit.

"Yeah I could go to uni in London of course. I haven't applied anywhere there but, you know, I could. I think it would break Robbie's heart if I didn't go. I can tell he daren't ask me to go with him, just in case I say no."

Oh whatever!!

As a bit of light relief the two Little Titches came skipping up. All titchy and excited. Ginger Titch said, "Miss Miss, we've got something to tell you. It's a secret."

I said, "Your library book's not a day overdue, is it?"

They shook their little heads. Then they did sort of "looking" at Wet Lindsay.

Then they did sort of "looking" to the science block. Ginger Titch said really quietly, "Follow us in a minute."

Then they did ludicrous waving and saying goodbye to me.

I wondered if they had been having Mad Miriam for theatre studies.

### One minute later

I scooted over to the science block. Wet Lindsay had seen me go, but she was too busy talking about her own no forehead or something to ADM.

The Titches nearly gave me a heart attack by leaping out from a rhododendron bush.

"Miss, quick, he's here. He wants you to go and see him. He's down at the back of school, by the lower playing-field fence."

My heart skipped. Blimey, this was a bit thrilling. I could tell him about Melanie Griffiths and...

That's when I realised I'd been thinking the Titches meant Dave the Laugh, but they meant the Luuurve God.

I did quick pouch work and hair bounceability and sloped off down the fields.

The afternoon sun glanced off the trees and their autumny leaves and then I saw him.

He smiled that wonderful smile of his. God, he's good-looking. He actually looks like a pop star.

He shouted, "*Cara*, I came round 'ere to the back, for not getting trouble. I had to see you. I rang you."

Have you ever kissed someone through a fence? I don't as such recommend it.

In fact, I think I may have slight fence burn on my mouth.

Which is unusual.

When I got back, the gang was agog (two gogs).

Rosie said, "So, what did he say?"

Ellen dithered into life. "Is he, will he, is he, are they???"

Jools said, "Go on, tell us everything."

I said, "Well, I dunno really. The Stiff Dylans have got a major management company now, but they have to be, you know, where it's all happening."

Ellen said, "Where, I mean is it... is it happening... here?"

I said, "Not as such."

Jas said, "So is it true, they are moving to London?"

I said, "That is the nub and gist."

Jas came and put her arm around me in a sudden lezzie attack. She said, "I know just how you are feeling. The Tom thing has made me know the meaning of heartbreak."

"Er, Jas, Tom's only going to pop over to Hamburger-a-gogo land for a week and a half. Masimo is moving to the throbbing metropolis."

Rosie said, "Oo-er."

The bell went for double physics. At least I can take my mind off things by amusing myself with Herr Kamyer.

Masimo wants to take me out to talk everything over tonight.

What is there to talk over though?

He has been asked to go to London for his career.

He's not going to not go, is he?

I am on the rack of luuurve again.

Marvellous.

## Double Physics

Two hours of unadulterated boredom and *merde*. If we

weigh atoms or whatever, I may eat my own head. Just to stop me being so bored.

Oh good, we are doing about "light". The only "light" in all of this is Herr Kamyer.

There is something so keen about him. Why? Has he just got the keenness gene? Mostly I think teachers come and teach because they hate us and want to make us suffer. But Herr Kamyer likes us. He does. If I had a conscience... well, I'd... well, I don't know what I would do. But thankfully I haven't.

To illustrate the difference between light and dark, Herr Kamyer had drawn the curtains and switched the lights off. Which was crap because it was still light outside and the curtains were see-through.

I said, "Herr Kamyer, we don't really experience dark any more, do we?"

He looked at me through his roundey glasses.

"*Ach zo*, Georgia, how do you mean zis?"

"Well... because of the lights in cities and you know global thingy and everything."

He said, "Global thingy?"

I said, "*Ja, ja*, zat is what I mean. We don't know what it is like to be in the dark."

He looked at me. "*Ja*, that is a *gut* point. No-vhere is completely dark."

I said, "Except for the photography dark room. Let's go in there and see what it is like to be completely in the dark."

Herr Kamyer said, "Vell, I don't know if..."

I got to my feet.

"*Ja, ja*, to the dark room."

The Ace Gang surged out, followed by the rest of the class.

The dark room is quite small and you could probably get about five people in comfortably. When we opened the door, it was quite literally pitch-black in there. Herr Kamyer stepped in and said, "*Ja*, now zen, girls if we go in maybe five at a time, we..."

At which point, all twenty-five of us crammed into the room and I slammed the door.

It was hysterical. I could hear Herr Kamyer, but I couldn't see a thing. It was just jampacked in.

And we were all shrieking and yelling, "Where am I?"

Herr Kamyer was shouting, "Now, ver is *der* door, girls? Calm down."

Then there would be the crash of some glass thing.

And the shrieking started again.

Rosie was shouting, "We're doomed, we're doomed!!!!!"

"Is that the door knob... oo-er."

Etc. etc.

After a few minutes of this, someone found the door handle and we piled out. Herr Kamyer came out last. His hair was all mussed up and his glasses were on sideways.

I couldn't stop laughing.

I said to him, "Now that is what I call dark."

### 5:00 p.m.

As I walked up our driveway, the mirthmobile was parked by the garage. Looking out of the back window was Bum-ty in his cage.

He is still up his ladder even though the cats are not around him. Mum must have left him in the car to give him a staring-free holiday.

### In my room

Masimo is coming at 7:00 p.m. I said I would meet him in town, but he insisted on picking me up. I am going to make sure I am waiting by the gate to avoid any chance of Dad "talking" to him.

I'm a nervy wreck.

I've already changed my clothes four times. I have to get out of my bedroom before I go mad.

## In the kitchen

Mum was doing her nails.

I could see Libby through the back window. She has got the washing-up bowl on the grass and is surrounded by Pantalitzer doll, Mr Fish and all her toys. She must be giving them a bath. She's obsessed with baths.

I said to Mum, "If someone really liked someone and had the chance to go off with them to somewhere really exciting, should they go?"

She looked at me.

"Someone really likes someone and wants to go off with them to somewhere really exciting."

Yes, yes, what is this? Simpletons' hour?

She was still rambling on though.

"And does this someone have any money to go off somewhere really exciting?"

"Not as such."

"Well, you can't go then, can you?"

Oh, she is so annoying. And unreasonable.

Half an hour later

I didn't mean to, but I have accidentally told Mum the whole story.

She was sort of not too bad about it.

In a bad way.

She said that she thought fifteen was too young to make a big commitment, away from home and away from your family and mates.

I said, "Well, I agree with the mates thing, but the family..."

She said, "And also, what will you be living on? Will your Luuurve God pay all the bills while you... erm... what is it you do exactly?"

I hate her and wish I hadn't told her anything.

I could just go.

She can't stop me.

What do the girlfriends of pop stars do actually?

I would miss the gang. Leaving all my pally wallys...

## Phoned Jas

"Jazzy, I'm sorry that I ever dissed your owls. And also your fire-making stick thing. It is well good."

Jas said, "What is this all about? I'm not going to get into any trouble, am I? You haven't got some new mad idea about papier mâché heads, have you?"

Oh, she is so full of suspicionosity.

I said, "No, it's just that I am on the horns of a dilemma vis-à-vis Masimo and I know I wasn't vair nice to you about Hunky going to Hamburger-a-gogo land."

Jas said, "Well, I know you didn't mean to be nice, but in fact you have been accidentally nice on purpose. I have told Tom that I want him to be happy and if he wants to go to college there, he should fly free and then we'll see what happens next. And he's going to go. "

"Jas, did you really set him free like a rubber band? Wow. And also wowzee wow wow."

Jas said, "I'm a bit freaky-deaky about it, but you can't stop people doing what they want. And anyway, I might go to York and see what it's like there. Apparently, they have a very active wildlife centre."

I said, "Steady on, Jas, are you hearing the call of the owl?"

Crikey. I think committing suicide on stage is bringing out the best in Jazzy.

I may spontaneously buy her Midget Gems tomorrow.

**7:00 p.m.**

Sitting on the gate waiting for the Luuurve God.

Oscar just came blundering up and said to me, and I quote, "Your legs must be tired because you've been running through my mind all night. Check it."

Dear *Gott in Himmel*.

I didn't say anything.

There is nothing to say.

It was getting a bit dark and nippy noodles. I'd compromised bikewear-wise by wearing a short skirt, but with thick tights and long boots. So hopefully, there would be no "gusset incident".

Masimo zoomed round the corner into my street. He had a leather flying jacket on. Which was vair cool.

He killed the engine on his bike and slowly took off his helmet. Then just sat on his seat looking at me. Sort of in an admiring way. Looking me up and down. Oh, good, my legs had gone all jelloid. I was going to fall off the wall and reveal my gusset before I even got on the bike.

I heard Oscar say, "Tosser".

And not in an ironic way seeing as it was coming from an absolute spoon.

Masimo just half turned in his seat and looked at Oscar. He said, "Ay you, monkey boy, vamoose."

And Oscar spat on the floor. (Why? Did he think Masimo was frightened of spit?) And then shuffled off, like he had meant to go anyway.

By the time Masimo got off his bike and came over to me, I had managed to gain some control of my legs.

Also I had remembered to wear my locket round my neck. Which was a lucky break because it was the first thing he kissed.

Er... was that odd?

Shut up, brain. Dave the Laugh has deffo started camping in my brain, twittering on about stuff. That is the problem with seeing too much of him. He gets in there with his annoying jokes. Although the boy's penid on the school playing field is, it has to be said, comedy gold.

I only wish I could tell the Luuurve God about it... but I can't.

## Five minutes later

We zoomed off and went to Ciao Bella's. Which is a quite groovy pasta place. In the centre of town. I've never actually been in it because it's quite new. And when we had passed it, I was with Dad, Libby and Grandad, and Dad said there was too much glassware around. And the waiters looked a bit too namby pamby to deal with Libby and Grandvati.

## one hour later

I suppose this is what my new Lunnern life will be like. Stopping off at bijou restaurants for a quick supper before... well, before what? Extended snogging?

The Luuurve God told me that the management people want them to move to London quite soon. Then he just looked at me and smiled. He touched my cheek.

"What do you think, Miss Georgia?"

Everyone is so bloody keen on me thinking all of a sudden. It's not what I do.

Masimo had tiny molluscs in spaghetti. Like little clammy things.

I'm bloody glad I had a pizza because if I had had

molluscs and spaghetti, I might have managed to choke and strangle myself at the same time. I feel like I am on the verge of an enormous visit to Strop Central, stopping only at nervy tiz headquarters.

Masimo said, "If you don't want me to go, I will not go. I can always do my music. Maybe I could write some songs for the band."

But it didn't seem right somehow.

He got hold of my hand.

"You are young – this is big decision for you. But, if you like, I will find for us a place to live. I have friends there, and you could go for your college there."

Go for college to do what?

**9:30 p.m.**

When I came in, Mum was mumming around.

She said, "Are you OK?"

I said, "What do you think?"

She said, "Would you like a hot choccy?"

"As if that will help."

"You do want one though, don't you?"

In the Kitchen

She went, "Sooo?"

I didn't mean to tell her, but I didn't have enough room left in my brain to think about it any more.

I said, "He said if I didn't want him to go, he wouldn't go."

She said, "Hmmm."

I said, "Mum, if you are going to annoy me by hhhhhmmmming I may as well go and tell some bees about it."

She put her arm around me.

"Look, I'm wanting to try and find out how you feel, that's all."

Well, she is not on her own there.

Mum says this is good practice for me, trying to figure out about love and how I feel.

She says I shouldn't be afraid to lose someone by saying the wrong thing.

She also said that girls make the mistake of thinking they should do what they think boys want.

After a while I said, "In a nutshell, Mum, are you saying that I should strop around doing what I want?"

She said, "Yep, boys like that. And also you will find that if you try to be good and nice and girlie and make sacrifices, you will get madder and madder at the boy. And he won't even know why."

### In my bedroom
What in the name of Beelzebub's Y-fronts is that supposed to mean?

### In bed
Why do I have to keep doing stuff?

Making decisions and so on.

It's bad enough knowing what shoes to wear but now, suddenly, it's all: What do you want to do as a job?

I don't know!! is the answer. I've only just really learned how to get up and go to school EVERY BLOODY DAY!!!

And now it's: Do you want to go to London and be a pop star's girlfriend?

I don't know!!! is the answer. It's only a minute and a half since I got a pop star. I don't know what you bloody do with them day after day.

I feel like stabbing something with my pretend sword.

Midnight

I can't wait for the swordfighting thing.

Maybe bludgeoning Ellen to death (metaphorically) will give me a bit of light relief.

# Whey-heyyyy!!

## Tuesday October 4th

Bum-ty has made a desperate bid for freedom! He is up the big tree next door.

Apparently Libby thought he needed a bit of a wash and blowdry, and got him out of the Robinmobile and into the washing-up bowl. When she went to get the hairdryer he must have staggered off.

He is free, free, free!!!!

Free from the cat staring.

He can fly free and wild with his sparrow friends.

As I walked to school, I could see lots of his sparrow friends all gathering on the branch near him.

Staring at him.

He is shuffling up the branches.

They are just staring.

## Stalag 14

### Ace Gang meeting

The gang are taking a vote on what I should do vis-à-vis the Luuurve God situation.

The options are:

a) Tell the Luuurve God not to go

b) Bravely tell him to go with a quivering lip (not him having the quivering lip, me having it... keep up)

c) Bog off to London with him and Devil take the hindmost. Our Lord Sandra will take care of me

d) The mysterious option d

It's a secret ballot paper, where you put a cross next to the option you choose.

However, I know which is Ellen's because she has ticked everything and then crossed it out and then ticked everything again.

OK, the result is: one vote for *c*. (That will be Rosie. In fact, I know it is because she put a cross with a little beard on it.) The rest are *b*s.

Sad really.

I sort of knew that would happen.

I said, "How come no one voted for the mysterious option *d*?"

Mabs said, "What is it?"

And I said, "I don't know. That is why it is so mysterious."

## Lunchtime

Jas had a secret rendezvous with Tom in the alleyway by the science block. I had to be the guardey dog type person.

That is the kind of top pal I am.

Actually, since she has decided to let Tom *boing* off on his elastic band she is getting quite un-Jasish. Less Miss Hufty Knickers and more Ms Loosey Goosey Knickers... With just a hint of Devil take the hindmost about the gusset area. She even applied a bit of lip gloss. In school hours!!! The little rebel. And she turned her skirt over. As she went off to meet Hunky, I said to her, "Jas, you're not wearing a thong, are you?"

And she didn't say no.

Or hit me.

Or fiddle with her fringe.

Hmmmmmm.

As I was lolling about, minding my own business, Elvis Attwood came shambling and perving along. With a hosepipe. He's probably pretending to clean the windows.

I said, "Your hosepipe is very big, Mr Attwood."

He, as usual, went sensationally ballistic for no reason.

He said, "Don't think I don't know what you're up to."

I said, "What am I up to?"

He said, "No good, that's what."

What kind of sense does that make? When he filled out his form to be a caretaker, they should have given him the lowdown about being a caretaker.

Stuff like, "If you take this job as caretaker at a girls' school, there will be quite a lot of girls there. At school. Do you see?"

It would have saved an awful lot of trouble.

I watched him turn the nozzle on the hose to start the water coming out. But nothing happened.

He really has got vair colourful language for a man who fought in the Boer War.

I watched him as he grumbled back along the hosepipe. He had got it wrapped round a bollard by mistake. He untangled it but then, with a huge *whoosh*, the trapped water came shooting out. The hosepipe snaked around like a bonkers python. A bonkers python that was chasing Mr Attwood. He was soaking wet before he managed to get to the tap.

Python hose even shot his hat off.

Quite, quite top entertainment.

The bell rang and Jas came scampering back going, "Oh, Hunky is sooo umm, I think I'll love him for ever no matter what happens..."

Yes, anyway, as we went back into the Temple of Doom, we saw Wet Lindsay slamming into the sixth-form common room. Phew, she was red and scary-looking.

I said to Jas, "What's the matter with her? Perhaps she tried to wear a hat today and it fell down over her eyes and she realised she has no forehead."

Jas looked a bit owly.

And tapped her nose.

What is that all about?

### Afternoon break

We've just heard on the Bush Telegraph, i.e. Jas, that Robbie has dumped Wet Lindsay. Tom told Jas that Robbie is deffo skipping off to London town with the band, but he is not taking the Wet Wipe with him. He has escaped from the slimy, slimy girl!!!!

Yessssss!!!!! And thrice Yessssssss!!!

### At the fives court

I said, "I think you will all agree that this is a victory in the fight against slimenosity. Robbie's bid for freedom calls for a celebration Viking bison disco inferno dance. But with a little added *je ne sais quoi*. In honour of the occasion."

So we did the Viking inferno dance, but at the end, instead of falling to our knees and yelling "Hoooorn", we yelled, "Duuuuuummmmmped!!!!!"

Which was slightly unfortunate timing, as Octopussy Girl herself and ADM came round the corner.

We sat down quickly and passed around refreshing Midget Gems. I looked at Lindsay and let a little smile play around my lips.

If looks could kill, I would have been deader than a dead

person on dead tablets. In dead land.

Wet Lindsay had tiny little mousey eyes from crying. I would feel a bit sorry for her, but she is such a mega cow and a half, and horrible to the Titches. And anyway, I've got used to hating her. It's a bit of light relief.

ADM was saying to her, "How do you feel?"

Wet Lindsay said, really loudly so that she was sure we would hear, "Well, to be honest, I let it happen. You know, I've sort of encouraged him to think he left me, but it's only to save his pride really. I mean when I went up to uni for my interview, there were loads of really fit boys there. Robbie is quite nice-looking, but there are better, much hotter boys."

What an enormously ludicrous Octopussy slime pot she was.

As we got up to go in, I looked at her and opened my eyes in a really ironic way.

She shouted at me, "And you can shut up, Georgia, you tart."

How can I shut up when I haven't said anything?

What is she going to do now – give me a reprimand for telepathic talking?

**6:00 p.m.**

Masimo called when I got home.

"*Cara*, I am off for meeting with the band. We are having talking about our plans, you know. How are you feeling?"

I said, "You know, a bit freaky-deaky."

"*Che...*"

"I mean I... oh, I don't know how to say it in Italian... but, well, I think it should be option **b**. On the whole."

In the end, the Luuurve God said he will pop round before his meeting to talk to me for a little while. Even if he can't understand what I am saying, it's still nice of him to come and see me.

**7:30 p.m.**

Sitting outside at the bottom of our garden in the dark. Masimo has put his coat around me and him, and we were looking up at the stars. Winking and a-blinking. But not giving any advice as such.

I even rescued Our Lord Sandra from Libby's teapot tonight. I've been looking for him/her for ages. I thought if I made a shrine for him, like I used to, it might help me know what to do. He had a BluTack foot before, but since I last saw him he seems to have lost a whole leg. I propped him up with Mr Potato Head. Libby doesn't lobe Mr Potato Head since he started going green, but I know Lord Sandra loves him... It doesn't say that he loved vegetables as such in the Bible. It doesn't say that he said "blessed are the leek", but he had whatsit, unconditional love, for all kind.

It was nice having him there. Still heavily rouged, it has to be said. But it doesn't alter his innernosity of goodness.

I suppose I didn't exactly have a conversation with him, but I did get the feeling that option ♭ would be the right thing to do.

Anyway, where was I? Oh yes. Masimo was being so sweet to me. When I look at him, I can't believe that he really likes me; he could have anyone he wanted. And actually, if he goes to London, he probably will.

Masimo said, "Georgia, Georgia."

And he kissed me softly on the mouth, and on the nose. (He's brave, I thought! Shut up, brain.) He was looking down at me.

"This for you is hard, but let me 'elp you."

I was glad to hear that because frankly I needed some 'elp.

He said, "This is how it is, for me. I have more years than you. I think, yes, it is *bene*, *molto bene*, that we have good offer for the band... but, I am man, I am good singer, another band will come." I started to say, "But I..."

He put his finger on my mouth.

"For you, it is big thing because you have not so many years. For you, you are afear that I will be sad not for to go to London. But no, for me is cool."

God, he was nice.

I started again, "But I..."

He said, "Let me finish, then you think more."

I nodded, but really I was thinking, Oh, good grief, please no more with the thinking. Cut my head off, please.

Masimo said, "I think if I go to London without you and say we will still be going out, you will be unhappy. You will not know where I am. You like big attention. You are big attention girl. You are like 'Me, me, me!!!'"

I thought er, no, I am not. I was only chatting with Lord Sandra earlier about the bestnosity of choosing option ♭.
But he didn't seem to think being a "Me, me, me" girl was a bad thing. He was smiling at me.

"Georgia, that is good. That is why I like you. But you

would be not good if I am busy always away from you. For me, I can say, 'I am your man, I will be thinking of you and no one else,' but you will not like. You will say, 'What about me, me, me!' "

Blimey.

When he said "Me, me, me", it really sounded like Libby. That's a bit alarming. I might be a me, me, me girl, but I'm not like Libby. I'm grown up. I haven't ever written BUM on a boy's forehead in indelible ink. (Although, to be honest, I am quite tempted to do it to Junior Blunder Boy.)

Shut up, brain. Concentrate.

Masimo had to go.

He said, "I think maybe I will be saying that, for me this time, I will not be going with the band. And that is for me good also. I will have you, and we will know each other, and then something else will happen. Later maybe we go to London together. *Ciao, bella.*"

I wanted to weep and weep. It was so sort of overwhelming.

And sort of grown up.

And sort of crap.

### In bed

Looking through my window into the night sky.

And at the tree next door.

I can't see Bum-ty anywhere.

### One minute later

The sparrows look a bit fatter to me.

Is this what happens when you do something wild?

You pay the price.

Is that what would happen to me if I went to London?

I would be eaten by cockney sparrows?

### Ten minutes later

Is Masimo actually going to give up his chance with the Stiffs for me?

Oooooooh I need someone to talk to about it.

If the Hornmeister could be bothered to keep in touch like a mate, I could ask him.

I think.

Actually, I'll be seeing him the day after tomorrow deffo because the "lads" are coming in after Stalag 14 for a tech read-through. Or "two hours of mayhem" as some people might call it.

I've learned my Merc-lurk-io part, which is a minor miracle given that he rambles on about the Queen of the Fairies for about a million years.

On the plus side, we are doing the swordfighting thing with Herr Kamyer tomorrow.

I may be able to work out my inner turmoil by whacking a big sword around. Oo-er.

## Wednesday October 5th
In the gym
Sword workshop

Herr Kamyer changed into his "sportswear" for the swordfighting. Although he kept his socks and sock suspenders on. We knew this because his trackie bums were ankle-length.

Miss Wilson practically bobbed her way to the loony bin she was so excited to have "Rudi" near her. She was saying, "Now pay careful attention to Herr Kamyer. He is the expert, and this needs to be very precise because it could be dangerous. Over to you, Herr Kamyer."

Rosie said, "She is deffo wearing Mivvy today."

Herr Kamyer took off his glasses.

We all went, "Ooooohhh, sir... why, you're beautiful," and so on.

"Now zen, girls, vat ve are doing *ist* choreographing ze fighting. Ve are not wildly waving our weapons around."

We all went, "Whey-heyyyyy!"

## Fifteen minutes later

Good Lord this is a larf. Nauseating P. Green has been stabbed twice and she isn't even in the fight scene. It's her arse; it just seems to attract the sword like a magnet.

Ellen (Tybalt... or something, er, what do you think) and me (Merc-lurk-io) have this fab fight backwards and forwards across the stage. Thrust, thrust, parry, thrust, thrust... "Oooh, sorry about that, Pamela"...thrust, thrust.

The only pity is that we are not allowed fake blood capsules. Miss Wilson said that, not only would it be slippery and dangerous, but that she thought it would be "more creative" for us to come up with our own artistic interpretation of blood being spilled.

Oh no.

Oh yes.

Fourteen minutes later

Of course it involves balloons and scarves. I knew it would. And free-form dance.

Dear God.

The village people come on when I am stabbed, with red balloons and scarves. Miss Wilson said, "Now then, you village people, you have become blood, you are blood. Blood corpuscles. Spilling out of the wound. Pumping and pumping! Wave those scarves and balloons. Interweave in a dance of blood and death."

Good Lord.

Nauseating P. Green said, "Should I still be the dog and blood at the same time?"

Miss Wilson said, "No, no, Pamela, put your dog on the side of the stage. You can leave it with one of the technicians."

I said to Rosie, "If it's Dave the Laugh she hands it to, she'll either never see it again or the next time she does see it, it will be wearing comedy glasses. Probably hers."

Oh, I am exhausted. The whole afternoon has been absolute top entertainment.

And I never thought I would say that about Stalag 14.

277

I'm full of exhaustosity, and even saying that is making me vair tired.

Gordy got stuck in a beer mug. Honestly. I don't know what to say.

Masimo called.

He sounded a bit down.

"*Ciao, cara.* Did you have good day?"

I said, "Yeah, we did swordfighting and it was tremendously crap. For the school play. *Rom and Jule.*"

He laughed. "Yes, I am glad you are more happy. I look forward to seeing you in it."

Oh no. No, no, no, no, no. Not in my tights. No.

Before I could say the no, no, no business he went on.

"The management, they call today, and they are upset. They say it might not be so good for the band. If I am not with them. I don't know. I say, Robbie he is good and they say yes, but it is more good with two."

Oh, bloody hell, now I was ruining six people's lives. Oh good.

Masimo is going off for another meeting with the band. Also he knows that Robbie has dumped Wet Lindsay.

I said, "Yes, well, every clud has a silver lining."

He didn't get it though.

**8:00 p.m.**

What should I do?

What if the management say that they won't take the Stiff Dylans without the Luuurve God? I would be the most hated girl in town since Big Fat Mary the Hateful. Whoever she was.

I wish I could talk to Dave the Laugh. It seems ages since I saw him.

I hope he hasn't got the hump with me again.

*It wasn't my fault he said I was beautiful.*

*I hadn't meant to be.*

*I'm not.*

**Looking in my mirror**

Especially as there is the suspicion of a lurker on my chin.

Oh no.

**In bed**

**8:15 p.m.**

Some absolute fool (Vati) has replaced Mr Fish's batteries.

Mr Fish is still singing "Maybe it's beCOD I'm a Londoner" and wriggling about. I said to Libby, "Turn him off now, he's tired."

Libby gave her mad heggy heggy ho laugh and said, "He's singing!!!"

I said, "I know he's singing, but it's time for bobos now. Let's tuck Mr Fish under the blankets so that he doesn't... erm... get..."

Libby said, "Fwightened."

"Yes, let's tuck Mr Fish up so he doesn't get frightened."

"Fwightened."

"Fwightened."

My life is a mockery of a sham of a fiasco.

Dreamt that I was fighting off lurkers.

It was disgusting actually.

I was in *Rom and Jule*, giving it my all in my tights, and the lurkers came lumbering and lurking up to me. Surrounding me. And when I hit them with a sword, they exploded like custard bombs. But they didn't give up; they just kept coming up to me all wriggling and exploding and singing... "Maybe it's because I'm a LURKERER!!!"

# Just call me Pongo

## Thursday October 6th
### French
Madame Slack had *le* nervy spaz today. She is vair highly strung. (Or should be.) We only laughed when we read in our *Français* textbook that the slang for a lady lavatory attendant was *une dame pipi*. And she started tutting and muttering in French.

She said we were childish.

*Caca* is to poo. Hahahahahaha.

To get her own back, she told us that the slang insult for English people is *Les Rosbifs* (the roast beefs) or *Les Biftecks* (the steaks).

Then she laughed like *le* drain.

I said to Rosie, "*Oooh là là*, she has really hurt my feelings now by saying I am a roast beef. I may never play the violin again."

What is the matter with the Froggy-a-gogo people?

### First technical run-through with the lads

I feel a bit nervy. I don't know why. The lads are due in a min. We are all huddled in the loos doing lippy work. Miss Wilson wanted us to wear our costumes. But in a fit of geniosity Jools said, "Miss Wilson, I think we should try and keep the, erm... mystery, and, er..."

I said, "Sheer bloody excitementosity."

Jools said, "Yes, keep the excitementosity down to a manageable level, by wearing casual clothes in rehearsal."

Essentially, what she is saying is that we will not be donning our tights in front of the lads until we absolutely have to.

Miss Wilson said, "Yes, yes, I see what you mean. Let the, the, mystery and excitement gather. Yes."

Of course, Jas was a bit miffed. She is keen as *la moutarde* to get into her Jule gear:

a) because she is a girlie swot and b) because she has a quite flattering dress to wear and a blonde wig. Which personally I like a LOT, due to its lack of fringeyness. I wonder what Jas will do with her hands when she hasn't got her fringe to fiddle with?

Try to fight off Melanie's basoomas, I should think. I don't think the binding is very secure on Rom's costume. When they last tried to strap her into her tunic, two buttons popped off and nearly blinded one of the villagers.

She must be a 34H if she is a day.

We are rehearsing with a ladder and a bit of scaffolding for the balcony scene... Mr Attwood is standing by with his first-aid kit. I bet he is hoping that Melanie strains a basooma and he has to put it in a splint.

Ten minutes later

Nauseating P. Green has brought some proper dog biscuits in for her puppet dog. Which she told everyone is called Pongo.

Jas said to P. Green, "I can't just call you Pongo you know. It's not in the script."

P. Green said, "No, but you will know that it's my name, and I will know it's my name."

I said, "Er, Pamela, how will we know it's your name if no one says your name?"

And Nauseating P. Green said, "I've got it on my dog collar."

And she has.

## 4:30 p.m.

The lads arrived.

We were all on the stage when they came in.

They sounded like they kicked the door open and all surged in at once. We sort of huddled at the back of the stage while they whooped and yelled.

I said to Rosie, "Can you see Dave the Laugh anywhere?"

And she said, "Are you having the General Horn?"

I said, "Nooo. I just can't see him and..."

At which point he walked in and waved at us all on the stage. He said, "Settle down, girls. I am here."

He went over to Miss Wilson and said, "May I say how thrilled I am that once more we can help you as you fill your Shakespearean tights."

Miss Wilson had a bit of a ditherspaz. Dave can look smiley and sincere while he says the rudest things.

She said, "Well, thank you, I, well, I am not, erm, filling, well I mean, I won't be, I'm not in the play of course. Would you boys start by looking at our lighting plan and the scenery that needs, erm, painting?"

Dave said, "Of course, sir. I have only the finest handpicked lads with me."

Fifteen minutes later

On the side of the stage, while Miss Wilson chalks stuff on the stage and so on.

Dave came up behind me. I had sort of felt too shy to go up to him and although he had caught my eye and winked, he was busy chatting to all the other girls.

He is an appalling flirt.

The girls were all giggling and being girlie.

Pathetico. I wonder if Emma would be so smiley if she could see him now.

He looked at me for what seemed like ages. Then he came really close to me. Oh my God. He said, "Hello, Miss. Show us your sword."

My head nearly fell off. Why does he come and stand so close to me?

285

I was so happy to see him though.

So I showed him my sword.

He said, "Ummm, groovy."

I said, "How did you manage to get handpicked?"

And he said, "Kittykat, as you know I am the vati. The vati is always handpicked, and the vati's mates are also handpicked."

I said, "Yes, yes, but who does the handpicking?"

And he said, "Hello."

**5:30 p.m.**

For a while, I forgot that I was on the horns of a whatsit. And also prob up shi cree without a padd.

As I predicted, when P. Green handed over Pongo to become a blood corpuscle, it was the last she saw of him. Until he appeared on the balcony with a false beard and a pair of comedy glasses at the suicide scene.

Actually, the lads were relatively well behaved. Probably because they were so mesmerised by Melanie's basoomas, especially when she tried to get up the ladder. They all offered to give her a hand up.

The *pièce de résistance* was, of course, the snogging scene.

You have never seen anything like it. Twenty lads at the side of the stage. All like seeing-eye dogs. I wouldn't mind, but it isn't even proper snogging. It's bloody mime snogging and they still were drooling like drooling droolers.

There is some crap music and then Jule and Rom start going into slow motion. Their eyes meet at the dance and then they walk over to each other. Then they pucker up really slowly: puckering and moving their heads from side to side, with their arms flailing about. And then there is the sound of waves crashing and they pretend to fall back and be swamped by the waves.

Then they do the slow-motion puckering and arms flailing thing again, and then the waves crash again and they fall back again.

It's WUBBISH snogging.

It's like in *Thunderbirds*, that crap puppet show, where you can see the strings, and the puppets' feet are about a metre off the ground.

However, in Melanie's case, it is not only the arms that are slow-motion flailing around. It is her nunga-nungas as well.

At the end of the big snogging fiasco all the lads went, "Phwoooaar."

As I have said, often, boys are sensationally weird.

### Twenty minutes later
Rosie got a bit of a telling-off for ad-hoc beard work during her Nursie scene.

As I have often said, she has two styles of acting: with or without the beard.

### Ten minutes later
My fight scene with Ellen was a triumph, dahling, a triumph.

At the end of it Dave the Laugh said to me, "I don't care what anyone says, I think you were marvellous."

### 6:30 p.m.
As we were all piling out of "rehearsal", Tom turned up in the hall. Jas went all pink, but amazed me by not dashing over to him like a simpleton. He came over to her and said, "I came to take you for a romantic walk in the woods."

And got hold of her hand and they walked off.

Ooohh. Quite touching really. If you like that sort of

thing. And also, it has to be said, Jas'n'Tom's idea of a "romantic walk in the woods" is almost bound to involve cuckoo spit.

As we were all going along the corridor to get out of Stalag 14, I was next to Dave the Laugh. All his mates were round so I didn't feel like I could say anything to him about the Luuurve God situation. But the lads were preoccupied with flirting and farting and so on, and it was Dave who said, "Gee, about the other night."

I said quickly, "I know, I know, you just said something nice to me, to make me feel nice... it's OK, I didn't really believe it. You were just like being nice or something."

Dave said, "Well... not exactly..."

I was thinking, oh no, he didn't mean it at all. He's embarrassed now.

I didn't know what to say.

He said, "I'm a bit confused."

I said, "You don't need to talk to me about confused, I am Lady Confused of... well, I don't know where..."

He said, "Look, I just wanted to say..."

I said, "No, I just wanted to say..."

By this time, we were outside going towards the gates.

Dave said, "Look, you've chosen Masimo and..."

I said, "Yeah, I know, but well..."

Dave said, "But well what..."

I didn't know what to say.

I said, "Just, yeah, I know, but well..."

Dave looked at me. He sighed. "God, Georgia..."

I said, "I know."

But I don't.

And that's when I saw Masimo waiting for me on his scooter.

Dave said, "You'd better go, Kittykat. I'm off to see Emma."

But he didn't sound pleased. He sounded sort of sad.

Oh double *merde*.

## Saturday October 8th

Jas phoned up.

"Gee, guess what? Dave the Laugh has finished with Emma."

What?

I said, "Really, how do you know?"

And she said, "Well, I've had Emma on the phone. She's

290

really upset. She couldn't speak at first. She just sort of hiccupped."

"Why did he say that he finished with her?"

"She said that he said that she was too good for him."

I said, "Well, to be frank, she is."

Jas said, "Yeah, but people always say that, don't they, when they dump people?"

Oh, here we go. Jas has gone back to her Wise Woman of the Forest ways.

I said, "Jas, forgive me if I'm right, but you have never been either the dumper or the dumpee, so how do you know so much?"

Jas was getting a bit numpty and I wanted to know all the juicy details so when she said, "I am a great observer of people," I didn't laugh or anything.

She was in full wisdomosity mood.

"Yes, it's like when you get dumped and people say, 'It's not you, it's me. I just need space.' And the space they need is exactly the height and width of the space that you are."

What is she on about?

I said, "What else did she say?"

Jas said, "Well, this is the weird bit, she said that he said there was someone else."

Ohmygod.

Someone else?

Dave had someone else?

And he said I was the most beautiful girl for him.

Whilst he had someone else?

Two someone elses.

# Twits in Tights fiasco

## Thursday October 13th
### Dress rehearsal
Dave wasn't at the dress rehearsal.

Jas said that Emma has been off school.

I didn't ask for any details, because I feel so weird about the whole Dave the Laugh multi-girlfriend scenario, but Radio Jas cannot help herself.

She said, "I went round to see her and she was in her dressing gown watching daytime TV and eating Pringles."

I said, "Well, that's all right, isn't it. My dad does that."

Jas said, "Yes, but does your dad have a picture of Dave

the Laugh pinned on to a teddy?"

Oh, bloody hell.

I said to Nursie, "Erm, aren't we supposed to be teenagers with not a care in the world etc.?"

Rosie said, "I haven't got a care in the world apart from an itchy beard."

I wonder if Dave the Laugh is off with his new mystery girlfriend?

He's a bit of a swine if he is.

Just dumping poor Emma and going off with someone else.

Without a care in the world.

Dumping Emma and telling me I am the most beautiful girl in the world.

Still, he is not my problem.

He has proved himself to be a hard-hearted Hornmeister and gad-abouty boy.

At Home
6:00 p.m.
Masimo is coming to the Twits in Tights fiasco.

Ooohh noooo.

I tried to persuade him not to, but he says he wants to see me.

In fact, even though I have once again tried to pretend to my family that the show is next week, they don't believe me.

Which is a savage indictment of our relationship in my opinion.

I said that to Mum. I said, "I am very upset that you don't trust me. If I tell you that the production is next week, why oh why do you not believe me?"

And she said, "Because I was talking to Jas's mum and she said she would see me there tomorrow night."

Oh, typical.

Jas has told her parents the proper night of the show. That is so typical.

She wants everyone to see her pretend snogging and being thrown around by pretend waves.

**6:30 p.m.**

Oh, fabulous... EVERYONE is coming.

Grandvati phoned up to tell me the wonderful news.

I answered the phone and he said, "Hello, hello, anybody there?"

295

And I said, "It's me, Georgia."

And he said, "Well, what do you want?"

Oh God's pyjamas and matching slipperettes.

I said, "Grandad, you phoned me."

He said, "Did I? What did I want?"

It turns out that he and Maisie (his knitted girlfriend) are coming along to see *Rom and Jule* as a special celebration.

I said, "You won't like it, Grandad, it's all mime and slow motion."

And Grandvati said, "Is that big girl in it again?"

**6:45 p.m.**

No amount of pleading will make my mutti and vati not come along. And they are bringing Libby. I said, "No, there is no need for that. She doesn't want to come."

I said that to her, "You don't want to come along to the silly old *Rom and Jule* thing, do you?"

She said, "I laiike it. I laiike Mr Cheese best."

I said, "Ah well, Mr Cheese is not in it."

She kicked me very hard on the ankle.

When I bent down to rub it, she put her little face in mine.

296

And went cross-eyed.

"Mr Cheese IS COMING!!! BAD GINGER!!!"

### One minute later

Oh, good, she is bringing Mr Cheese.

And Mr Fish, probably.

### Five minutes later

Oh, well, maybe it will be all right. I'm only on for about a minute anyway and then I can just lurk around annoying Mr Attwood, or trying to put Jule off with my amusing backstage pranks (which she will then kill me for).

### 8:00 p.m.

Masimo phoned again.

He sounds vair miz.

He said, "I 'ave been with the band all day. It is sad. They are my, how do you say it, mates now. I will be not having them for my mates when they go to London."

I said, "Oh, Masimo. Look, why, well, why... don't you, why don't you go with them? For a bit? To London."

There was a silence.

He said, "You want me to go?"

"No, no, it's just that you seem so unhappy, and..."

"But you will not come with me."

"I think, I am too... I don't think I have enough..."

"Money? I can get the money."

"No, I don't think I have enough... maturiosity."

"Mat... nosity? What is this?"

Then I sort of had a brainwave (ish) well, a brainripple anyway.

"It's just I don't want to leave my mates either. I have special mates and I don't want to leave them."

He said, "I understand, Georgia. I so like you, *cara*."

Oh, bloody blimey and also pooooooooooooooooo.

Why can't everything be simple???

## In the front room

The Blunder Boys are having a "gathering". Just outside our front-room window.

Mark Big Gob is clearly the lovechild of Mick Jagger and a cod. His gob is huge.

I can't hear what they are saying, thank God. It's just odd words like "wicked" and "yeh mon" and I did hear Oscar say,

"She wan' me baaaaaad."

As if.

Also they were doing that really crap boy smoking. You know, holding the fag upside down and taking really big drags on it.

Angus hopped up on to the windowsill and was looking at them.

Doing his staring thing.

When they noticed him, I could hear them going on.

"Look at the stupid cat. He is rank."

"Hey, stupid cat, want to kiss my arse?"

On and on.

Angus was just looking and looking at them.

Ten minutes later

He is still looking at them.

But they are not saying anything.

In fact, they are looking a bit shifty.

Two minutes later

They have all shuffled off somewhere else.

Yes!!!!!

Super cat scores again!

He has quite literally outstared them.

## In bed

Dear Lord Sandra, please give me some advice.

What shall I do about Masimo?

## Three minutes later

I have decided that I am going to remove Mr Potato Head and if Lord Sandra falls over, that is a sign that I should tell Masimo that he should go to London.

If Lord Sandra stays upright, then I should have a full-on relationship with the Luuurve God.

## Five minutes later

What does it mean if Lord Sandra just leans slightly to the left?

# Rom and Jule: the tragedy (you're not kidding, mate)

## Friday October 14th
### Final run-through

We're giddy with excitement (ish).

Jas was asking me about her puckering technique.

She said, "Does this look like real snogging?"

And made a little face like a fish.

I said, "Jas, if that is how you snog Tom, I am not surprised he is high-tailing it to Hamburger-a-gogo land."

She stropped off because she seems to forget that we are bestie mates of all time, weathering the storms of luuurve

♡ 301

together. She seems to have forgotten that.

That and her emergency supply of Midget Gems, which I am looking after for her.

I have to give her one when she comes off stage in between scenes, so that she has the courage to face her audience.

Good Lord.

I wonder if Dave the Laugh will turn up tonight.

I bet he feels horrible about Emma.

Maybe he is consoling himself with his mysterious girlfriend.

Not that it is any of my business.

### 11:00 a.m.

I cannot believe this place. Us artistes are being made to do ordinary lessons. How can that be right? We need to be limbering up. Stretching our vocal cords and our tights etc.

### Maths

Miss Stamp does not seem to understand that my answers are meant ironically.

Lunchtime

Lolling around trying to conserve our strength.

Wet Lindsay came sliming by. Hasn't she died yet?

She said, "What a bloody bunch of losers and liggers you are."

Charming.

I said, "Actually, we are trying to relax before this evening's gala performance."

She didn't even bother to reply.

Rosie said, "Better to have loafed and lost than never to have loafed at all."

Lindsay turned round then.

She said, "What is that supposed to mean, Mees?"

Blimey, was there going to be a fight?

By the way, although people suggest the youth of today do not pay attention to boring stuff, I will just say this. The French for a fight between two girls is *un crêpage de chignons* (a fight between hairstyles).

I said to Rosie, "Are you going to be having *un crêpage de chignons* as a warm-up for tonight's fiasco? Don't ruin your beard."

But then Wet Lindsay just turned away and said, "You're not worth it."

And stormed off.

But fortunately for us, she stumbled on the top step of the science block.

I said, "If you fall down those stairs and break your legs, don't come running to me!"

Oh, we laughed. But quietly.

Sort of quietly but hysterically at the same time.

Jas said, "Emma said that she might turn up tonight."

Oh dear God.

What if she flung herself on stage and grabbed my sword?

### 7:30 p.m.
### Showtime!!!
The roar of the greasepaint, the smell of the crowd.

### Backstage
Jas was pacing backwards and forwards. And even though she has no fringe on her wig, she is still managing to fiddle about with her forehead. It is vair annoying.

She said, "Do you think everyone will know it's a tragedy?"

I said, "I guarantee tonight that after our moving interpretation of *Rom and Jule*, there will not be a dry seat in the house."

Especially as my grandvati and Libby are coming and they have trouble in the piddly-diddly department. But I didn't say that bit to Jas.

No sign of Dave the Laugh. He must really be having a bad time.

I hope he is all right, even if I am eschewing him with a firm hand because of his new secret girlfriend that I don't even care about.

**7:31 p.m.**

Dave the Laugh turned up.

He looked a bit dark around the eyes, like he hadn't slept much. But he greeted all his mates with the usual slapping and "You idiot" sort of carry on.

He saw me and said, "Nice tights, Kittykat... and enormous beard."

I didn't mean to talk to him. I was going to give him my cold-shoulderosity work for being a cad and a bounder but unfortunately I couldn't help smiling at him.

Actually, even though he looked tired, he did look really lovely.

After he had been joshing around with the others he came over to me and said, "All right, Kittykat?"

And suddenly, I felt like crying. I wanted him to just get hold of me.

I said, "Well, not really. It's all been a bit..."

He said, "I know, it really has been all a bit... but come on, gird your gusset and cheer up. It will be all right. The Hornmeister is here."

### By the side of the stage
Melanie has done her best as Rom, but she is struggling against enormous odds (oo-er).

As soon as she came on, I could hear my grandad say, "Bloody hell, she's a mature lass."

She did her best, but she is not really an actress as such.

In fact, as Dave the Laugh said, "The only thing moving about her performance is her wig."

Every time Nauseating P. Green came on as the puppet dog,

I could hear Libby howling with laughter. And unfortunately, I could see her howling with laughter. This was because she had three seats to herself on the front row. One for her, Pantalitzer doll, Scuba-diving Barbie and burnt-bottom Panda, one for Mr Fish and one for Mr Cheese. Mr Cheese was not naked as he is at home – he had on his lovely macintosh.

Ramble ramble *Rom and Jule.*

At last it was my big fight scene. I took a deep breath and adjusted my beard.

Before I went on, Dave gave me the thumbs up and said, "Give it your all tightswise! I'm right behind you, oo-er."

### Onstage

My dying was another triumph darling, a triumph! I even improvised recovering a bit, just when everyone thought I was a goner.

I could see Dave the Laugh by the lighting console, rubbing his hands like he was a masterchef or something. The lights dimmed to atmospheric red and through my half-closed eyes I could see the "blood corpuscles" dancing up to me like twits and waving their red scarves about.

Then, as last year, once again the stage was plunged into complete darkness.

I couldn't see a bloody thing. I heard someone whisper (loudly), "Which way is off?" then there was a bit of a bang and someone in the dark said, "Bloody hell, what's that?" and then Mr Attwood's voice saying very loudly, "You've just put your foot in my first-aid kit."

It was an absolute shambles.

I stood up and started sort of shuffling along sideways in the dark when the lights suddenly came up again.

I could see the audience quite clearly.

Looking at me.

I thought about doing some Irish dancing but it didn't seem right somehow. I kept on shuffling because I couldn't just lie down again. Then someone shouted out, and I am pretty sure it was my dad, "It's a bloody miracle. He's alive!!!" And the audience applauded, so me and the blood corpuscles had to bow.

Backstage
I looked at Dave the Laugh and he shrugged and said, "Technical hitch but the show must go on, Kittykat."

He has no shame.

Also he said it was an accident waiting to happen.

I said, "What was?"

And he said, "Putting me in charge of lights."

Miss Wilson went bobbing out on to the stage and said, "Erm, despite the erm, technical hitch, erm we will carry on... please ignore the erm, Mercutio walking off. He is in fact dead."

I could hear Dad and Uncle Eddie booing.

The next scene was Melanie's big climbing on to the balcony scene. All of the lads crowded round the sides of the stage. The atmosphere was so stiff with hormones I could have cut it with my sword. But sadly, I had broken it trying to open a bottle of lemonade backstage.

Melanie put her foot on the lower rung of the ladder and then reached out to haul herself up to the next rung. All of the lads and the audience went "Oooooooohhh" and then she went for the next rung and they all went "Oooooooohhh". It was riveting to watch.

Finally, she got to the balcony and hauled herself up on to it. As she stood up and opened her arms to speak, all the buttons on her tunic pinged off. And as she looked down in horror, Dave the Laugh said really loudly, "Are these my basoomas I see before me?"

After show

I like to think the play was a unique experience for everyone. Lots of people came backstage and said they had quite literally never seen anything like it.

We were all doing a mad conga backstage, wearing beards, when Masimo came in.

I had completely forgotten he was coming.

I felt so awful.

He looked at me in my beard with Dave the Laugh and the others.

Oh no.

He wasn't going to challenge Dave the Laugh to another fisticuffs at dawn, was he?

I wouldn't really blame him this time.

In fact, I would lend him my handbag.

Shut up, brain.

Then he smiled at me.

It was a really lovely smile.

I went over to him and he said to me, "*Cara*, can

we talk for a minute? Not too long away from your friends."

And he wasn't being mean or anything, just really lovely and soft.

We went off down the corridor and through the fire exit to the outside. Which was great as I thought my head was going to explode into flames.

He looked at me and stroked my face.

Thank God I had quickly removed my beard.

He said, "Georgia, I am going to say this, for you. I am going for London. I will go, now, tonight."

I went, "But, but..."

And he said, "I don't think I can speak long, for my heart. But I see how this is for you. I know you like me much, but you are, your heart is here. I will not make you choose. I am going. Be happy. I do not think I will ever meet anyone like you again... *Ciao*."

And he gave me the longest, softest kiss. I couldn't speak. My head had frozen over.

And he just went.

I should run after him. I should say something.

But.

I went back into the theatre. Like I was in a soup. I sat down by the loos.

How did I feel?

I don't know.

I must have been sitting there for about five minutes when Jas came out.

She saw me and came over to me.

First of all she was saying, "People cried when I died." Blah blah ramble ramble.

But then she stopped and said, "Gee, what is it?"

I said, "Masimo has gone off to be with the Stiff Dylans in London."

She put her arm about me.

"Oh, Gee. How do you feel?"

I said, "I dunno; funny."

She said, "Oh I'm sorry. You've liked him for ages, I know. And he is lovely. I know I said the Dave thing but I think you really were right to like him, but..."

I looked up at her and even though she was fiddling with her wig, I didn't mind.

I just said, "But what?"

She looked a bit thoughtful.

"Well he always made you nervous, and you know, we're only like, well we're not like Jule, are we? I mean, we aren't going to get married, are we? Just yet... or... well, I think we need our pals. And we need to grow up a bit together. Like a little family."

I looked at her.

"I would really miss you if you weren't here, Jas."

She said, "I know, and I would really miss you."

And she gave me a big hug.

Then she said, "We'll be all right, little pally. I bet you something really nice will happen now. It will all work out in the end."

I said, "How do you know that?"

And she said, "I don't know, it just does. Do you want a Midget Gem?"

I nodded. I did quite want one as it happened.

She went off and I just sat there again.

I was looking down at the floor when I heard her coming back again.

I said, "Can I have the black one?"

And Dave the Laugh said, "You cheeky minx."

I looked up at him.

313

He said, "Jas told me."

I looked at him.

He has the loveliest smile.

I said to him, "You said 'Are these my basoomas I see before me,' and everyone heard you."

He said, "I know, I am the vati."

I said, "Yeah, you are the double-timing vati."

He said, "What do you mean?"

"You know, your secret girlfriend that you dumped Emma for."

He looked at me.

"You may be the thickest chick alive. You're the secret girlfriend, you daft tart."

And he kissed me.

I said, "So, do you, want to be my girlfriend? I mean, do you want to..."

He put his arm around me.

"Go on then, Sex Kitty, I'll be your girlfriend. It'll probably all end in tears. Mine. But... I am Dave the Biscuit. I will survive. Give us a snog and possibly a *rummachen unterhalb der Taille*. Go on, you know you want to."

And I did want to.

## The end

So as Billy Shakespeare said, "Forsooth and verily all endeth happily in the snogging department."

Probably.

Or something?

What do you think?

I'll be the last to know.

# Georgia's Glossary

**bhaji** · A bhaji is an Indian food. An onion bhaji is brown and round and full of fat, hence my hilarious joke about Slim looking like one. I exhaust myself with my good humour, I really do.

**Blimey O'Reilly** · (as in "Blimey O'Reilly's trousers") This is an Irish expression of disbelief and shock. Maybe Blimey O'Reilly was a famous Irish bloke who had extravagantly big trousers. We may never know the truth. The fact is, whoever he is, what you need to know is that a) it's Irish and b) it is Irish. I rest my case.

**BluTack** · Blue plasticine stuff that you stick stuff to other stuff with. It is very useful for sticking stuff to other stuff. Tip-top sticking stuff actually. I don't know why it's called BluTack when it clearly should be called Blue Sticking Stuff. Also, blue is spelt wrong, but that's life for you.

**bobos** · As I have explained many, many times, English is a lovely and exciting language full of sophisticosity. To go to sleep is "to go to bobos", so if you go to bed you are going to Boboland. It is an Elizabethan expression... Oh, OK then, Libby made it up and she can be unreasonably violent if you don't join in with her.

**brillopads** · A brillopad is a sort of wire pad that you clean pans and stuff with (if you do housework, which I sincerely suggest you don't. I got ironer's elbow from being made to iron my vati's huge undercrackers). Where was I? Oh yes. When you say "It was brillopads" you don't mean "It was a sort of wire pad that you clean with," you mean "It was fab and groovy." Do you see? Goodnight.

**Bugger(ation)** · A swear word. It doesn't really mean anything but neither do a lot of swear words. Or parents.

**bum-oley** · Quite literally "bottom hole". I'm sorry but you did ask. Say it proudly (with a cheery smile and a Spanish accent).

**catsuit** · An all-in-one suit thing with trousers and a zipper up the front. Usually evening wear. It is supposed to be sexy, and perhaps it is, but try getting out of one quickly if you have to pay an emergency lavatory call. Like a grown-up version of a romper suit.

Chuntering · When people are moaning on, they are said to be "chuntering". An example of chuntering would be my dad saying, "Why can't you tidy your room like a normal person. I found two pizzas and a dog bone in there that must have been there for weeks. A decent person would tidy their room. An ordinary person... blah blahh chunter chunter."

clown car · Officially called a Reliant Robin three-wheeler, but clearly a car built for clowns by some absolute loser called Robin. The Reliant bit comes from being able to rely on Robin being a prat. I wouldn't be surprised if Robin also invented nostril-hair cutters.

clud · This is short for cloud. Lots of really long boring poems and so on can be made much snappier by abbreviating words. So Wordworth's poem called "Daffodils" (or "Daffs") has the immortal line "I wandered lonely as a clud". Ditto *Rom and Jule*. Or *Ham*. Or *Merc of Ven*.

**Dark room** · Oh stop being so lazy – you know what a dark room is. It's a room. And it's dark. Leave it. Leave the dark room.

**div** · Short for "dithering prat", i.e., Jas.

**DIY** · Quite literally "Do It Yourself"! Rude when you think about it. Instead of getting someone competent to do things around the house (you know, like a trained electrician or a builder or a plumber), some vatis choose to do DIY. Always with disastrous results. For example, my bedroom ceiling has footprints in it because my vati decided he would go up on the roof and replace a few tiles. Hopeless.

**Epée** · A form of swordfighting. All swordfighting is hilarious, but *épée* takes the biscuit comedywise because: a) there is a comedy opportunity for misunderstanding that someone is not actually saying... a pee, and b) when you fight with an *épée* it is a sword with a bit on the end so that you cannot hurt anyone. Which has to be one of the most pointless things around. (Do you see? Do you see what I did there? "Pointless." Do you see? Oh, I am so vair vair tired.)

**fives court** · This is a typical Stalag 14 idea. It's minus forty-five degrees outside so what should we do to entertain the schoolgirls? Let them stay inside in the cosy warmth and read? No, let's build a concrete wall outside with a red line at waist height and let's make them go and hit a hard ball at the red line with their little freezing hands. What larks!

**fringe** · Goofy short bit of hair that comes down to your eyebrows. Someone told me that American-type people call them "bangs", but this is so ridiculously strange that it's not worth thinking about. Some people can look very stylish with a fringe (i.e. me) while others look goofy (Jas). The Beatles started it (apparently). One of them had a German girlfriend and she cut their hair with a pudding bowl, and the rest is history.

**f.t.** · I refer you to the famous "losing it" scale:

1. minor tizz
2. complete tizz and to-do
3. strop
4. a visit to Stop Central
5. f.t. (funny turn)

6. spaz attack
7. complete ditherspaz
8. nervy b. (nervous breakdown)
9. complete nervy b.
10. ballisticisimus

**gadzooks** · An expression of surprise. Like for instance, "Cor, love a duck!" Which doesn't mean you love ducks or want to marry one. For the swotty knickers among you, "gad" probably meant "God" in olde English and "zooks" of course means... Oh, look, just leave me alone, OK?

**geoggers** · Geoggers is short for geography. Ditto blodge (biology) and lunck (lunch).

**gob** · Gob is an attractive term for someone's mouth. For example, if you saw Mark (from up the road who has the biggest mouth known to womankind) you could yell politely, "Good Lord, Mark, don't open your gob, otherwise people may think you are a basking whale in trousers and throw a mackerel at you!" Or something else full of hilariosity.

**goosegog** · Gooseberry. I know you are looking all quizzical now. OK. If there are two people and they want to snog and you keep hanging about saying, "Do you fancy some chewing gum?" or "Have you seen my interesting new socks?" you are a gooseberry. Or for short, a goosegog, i.e. someone who nobody wants around.

**gusset** · Do you really not know what a gusset is? I do.

**Hoooorn** · When you "have the Horn" it's the same as "having the big red bottom".

**On my jacksie** · It means on my own. All aloney. On my owney. It is of course Olde Englishe and was formed because "jacksie" rhymes with... erm... alonesie.

**Jammy Dodger** · Biscuit with jam in it. Very nutritious(ish).

**jimjams** · Pyjamas. Also pygmies or jammies.

**Knickers** · Americans (wrongly) call them panties. Knickers are a particular type of "panty" – huge and all encompassing. In the olden days (i.e., when Dad was born) all the ladies wore massive knickers that came to their knees. Many, many amusing songs were made up about knicker elastic breaking. This is because, as Slim, our headmistress, points out to anybody interested (i.e., no one), "In the old days people knew how to enjoy themselves with simple pleasures." Well, I have news for her. We modern people enjoy ourselves with knicker stories too. We often laugh as we imagine how many homeless people she could house in hers.

**Le Coq** · Hahahahahahahaha. Do you see why this is so funny??? For the same reason that the Koch family are so funny. *Le Coq* is alarmingly, the name of a mime school in *le gay* Paree. People go there to learn how to look as though they are trapped behind a glass wall etc. No one knows why.

**Leper of Rheims** · Oh come on, you must know who the Leper of Rheims is. Oh blimey. Well. He was living in Rheims – erm – in ancienty times and he had dodgy skin. And as we all know the Rheims-type people (the Rheimsonians) can't abide a poor complexion so they ignored him. The end.

**loo** · Lavatory. In America (land of the free and criminally insane) they say "rest room", which is funny, as I never feel like having a rest when I go to the lavatory.

**Merc-lurk-io** · a.k.a. Mercutio. He is Rom's friend in *Rom and Jule* and supposed to be the "comedy" element in the tragedy. But as far as I can see, he just hangs around in a lurking way. Hence my vair vair amusant nickname. Occasionally, he stops lurking to fight and complain. Much like my vati.

**Midget Gem** · Little sweets made out of hard jelly stuff in different flavours. Jas loves them A LOT. She secretes them about her person, I suspect, often in her panties, so I never like to accept one from her on hygiene and lesbian grounds.

**nippy noodles** · Instead of saying "Good heavens, it's quite cold this morning," you say "Cor, nippy noodles!!" English is an exciting and growing language. It is. Believe me. Just leave it at that. Accept it.

**nub** · The heart of the matter. You can also say gist and thrust.

This is from the name for the centre of a wheel where the spokes come out. Or do I mean hub? Who cares. I feel a dance coming on.

**nuddy-pants** · Quite literally nude-coloured pants, and you know what nude-coloured pants are? They are no pants. So if you are in your nuddy-pants you are in your no pants, i.e. you are naked.

**nunga-nungas** · Basoomas. Girls breasty business. Ellen's brother calls them nunga-nungas because he says that if you get hold of a girl's breast and pull it out and then let it go, it goes nunga-nunga-nunga. As I have said many, many times with great wisdomosity, there is something really wrong with boys.

**Och Aye land** · Scotland. Land of the Braves. Or is that Indiana? I don't know, and I know I should because we are, after all, all human beings under our skins. But I still don't care.

**Pantalitzer doll** · A terrifying Czech-made doll that sadistic parents (my vati) buy for their children, presumably to teach them early on about the horror of life.

**Pizza-a-gogo land** · Masimoland. Land of wine, sun, olives and vair vair groovy Luuurve Gods. Italy. The only bad point about Pizza-a-gogo land is their football players are so vain that if it rains, they all run off the pitch so that their hair doesn't get ruined.

**red-bottomosity** · Having the big red bottom. This is vair vair interesting *vis-à-vis* nature. When a lady baboon is "in the mood" for luuurve, she displays her big red bottom to the male baboon. (Apparently he wouldn't have a clue otherwise, but that is boys for you!!) Anyway, if you hear the call of the Horn, you are said to be displaying red-bottomosity.

**rucky** · A rucksack. Like a little kangaroo pouch you wear on your back to put things in. Backpack.

**sailor's hornpipe** · As I have pointed out many, many times, England is a proud seafaring nation and our sailors on the whole are jolly good chaps etc. However, when they were first invented in the olden days, they had a few too many rums and made up this odd dance called a "hornpipe", which largely consists of hopping from foot to foot with your arms crossed. Well, you did ask.

**Scheissenhausen** · Quite literally (if you happen to be a Lederhosen-type person) a house that you poo in (*scheiss* is poo and *haus* is house). Poo house. Lavatory. Or rest room as Hamburger-a-gogo types say. No one knows why they say that. Oh no, hang on, I think I do know. When they all lived in the Wild West in wooden shacks, one room was both their bedroom and their lavatory. Cowboys didn't mind that sort of thing. In fact they loved it. But I don't.

**Silly beggars** · Playing "silly beggars" is an old-fashioned term used by the elderly insane, when they are suggesting that the youth of today are acting stupidly. Which of course, as we all know, they never do.

**Sing-alonga** · This is when you have the lyrics to songs printed along the bottom of a film. So that the audience can sing along. (Not the lyrics to any songs... just the lyrics to the songs in the film. Otherwise you would be there all day and night.)

**Spoon** · A spoon is a person who is so dim and sad that they cannot be allowed to use anything sharp. That means they can only use a spoon. The Blunder Boys are without exception all spoons.

**Strawberry Mivvy** · Is an ice lolly. It has red-coloured ice on the outside but inside (when you have sucked like a mad sucking thing) you find the ice cream centre. Hurrah!! People who eat them usually end up with red lips and chin. Often with a slight red moustache effect. Miss Wilson of course took it the whole hog and managed to get red nostrils. Either that or she had applied lippy in the dark with a spoon.

**The Sound of Music** · Oh, are we never to be free? *The Sound of Music* was a film about some bint, Julie Andrews, skipping around the Alps and singing about goats. Many, many famous and annoying songs come from this film, including, "The Hills Are Alive With the Sound of PANTS", "You Are Sixteen Going on PANTS" and, of course, the one about the national flower of Austria, "IdlePANTS".

**Titches** · A Titch is a small person. Titches is the plural of titch.

**tosser** · A special kind of prat. The other way of putting this is "wanker" or "monkey spanker".

**vino tinto** · Now this is your actual Pizza-a-gogo talk. It quite literally means "tinted wine". In this case the wine is tinted red.

**waz** · Another expression for piddly-diddly department. Possibly named after the sound the piddly diddly makes as it comes out of the trouser area. I don't know, to be frank. Only boys say it. And who knows why boys say anything? The whole thing is a mystery.

**wazzarium** · A place where you go to have a waz.
p.s. You will not be finding me in there.

**welligogs** · Wellington boots. Because it more or less rains all the time in England, we have special rubber boots that we wear to keep us above the mud. This is true.

**whelks** · A horrible shellfish thing that only the truly mad (like my grandad, for instance) eat. They are unbelievably slimy and mucuslike.

**Wild Thing** · This is a 60s song sung by a band called The Troggs. It is about a wild thing. That is how simple life was in the 60s. If you had a Wild Thing now (which believe me, I do) people would not say it was groovy, they would put a restraining order on it.

# The Having the Hump Scale

1. ignorez-vousing

2. sniffing *(in an I-told-you-so way)*

3. head-tossing and fringe-fiddling

4. cold-shoulderosity work

5. Midget Gems all round, but not for you

6. pretendy deafnosity

7. walking on ahead

8. the quarter humpty *(evils)*

9. the half humpty *(evils and withdrawal of all snacks)*

10. the Full Humpty Dumpty *(walking away with dignitosity at all times)*

# The Snogging Scale

1/4. Kissing hands

1/2. sticky eyes (*Be careful using this. I've still got some complete twit following me around like a seeing-eye dog.*)

1. holding hands

2. arm around

3. goodnight kiss

4. kiss lasting over three minutes without a break (*What you need for this is a sad mate who's got a watch but no boyfriend.*)

4 1/2. hand snogging (*I really don't want to go into this. Ask Jas.*)

5. open mouth kissing

6. tongues

6 1/2. ear snogging

6 3/4. neck nuzzling

7. upper body fondling - outdoors

8. upper body fondling - indoors

Virtual number 8. (*When your upper body is not actually being fondled in reality, but you know that it is in your snoggees head.*)

9. below waist activity (*or bwa.*)

10. the full monty (*Jas and I were in the room when Dad was watching the news and the newscaster said, "Tonight the Prime Minister has reached Number 10." And Jas and I had a laughing spaz to end all laughing spazzes.*)

# Great Mates Scale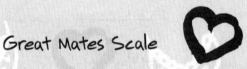

1. Offer a mate a Midget Gem without being asked.

2. Share your last Jammy Dodger even though you really want it and your mate may be flicking her fringe about.

3. Listen to your mate rambling on about themselves when you have got vair important things to do yourself (e.g. nails, plucking etc.).

4. Be with your mate through thick and thin. Or even if they are both thick and thin.

5. Always be game for a laugh even though you may be blubbing on the inside.

6. Even when they have all the reason in the universe to be Top Dog (i.e. when they are the girlfriend of a Luuurve God, even if it is slightly on a sale-or-return basis) a top mate does not blow their own trumpet. Or snitch on her less fortunate mates.

scottish wildcat association

# The brethren of Angus

Up in Och Aye land, there is a nature reserve where they are trying to look after the Scottish wildcats and breed them up a bit. Please let us save them, there are only 400 left and they have been in Och Aye land for thousands of years.

The bestiest news is that they are probably Vikings. They came from the North of Europe to Scotland and I am just guessing, but I bet they wore little horned helmets as they paddled across to our land.

They have an overhead run in the trees, like a cage tunnel and they scamper around up there because they like to be

above people. When it is feeding time, they come down from the trees and into a central caged off bit to eat dead chicks and rabbit legs and so on.

Scottish wildcat kittens pretty much lay waste to anything they can get at, leaping on leaves and twigs and wrestling with them etc. They also luuurve doing flying face-pouncing and grabbing on to each other with their front paws to do bunny kicks with their back legs.

Their *pièce de resistance* is staring at things. And one paw clapping; two kittens standing on their back legs and biffing in the direction of each other with one paw.

Find out more about Scottish wildcats at:
www.scottishwildcats.co.uk